He didn't know what else to say. Or how to explain it—even to himself.

So, instead, he did the only thing he knew how to do—he kissed her.

Over and over.

Pouring everything he had into the moment. All the words he couldn't bring himself to think, let alone say. All these...*feelings* that he didn't know how to even begin to unravel.

As if Nell Parker was the only thing that could make this darkness inside him shift and skitter. As if he was running toward the light that this one unique woman brought into his life. She flooded him with it, bright and brilliant as it illuminated all the better versions of himself that he wished he could be. For her.

And, for a while at least, he could pretend to himself that he really was that better man. Something he'd never wanted to believe in so much in his entire life.

Dear Reader,

When I first began to imagine Nell and Connor's story, it was the character of Connor who roared into my head—on that supersleek, powerful motorbike of his, of course—and onto that country lane overlooking the Meadwood valley.

It wasn't difficult to work out that it had to be a significant event that had made him return after so many years, but what proved more challenging was understanding why Nell had never left. What reason could she possibly have for never spreading her wings to fly?

She was such a bubbly, happy, caring heroine that it took me a while to understand the fears simmering beneath the surface—and even then, it only happened when she was with her best friend, Ruby.

I had a blast writing Nell and Connor's story, and I hope you truly love reading it—but you'll have to excuse me...I just can't wait to dig into Ruby's own story!

Charlotte x

TRAUMA DOC TO REDEEM THE REBEL

CHARLOTTE HAWKES

ISBN-13: 978-1-335-94255-5

Trauma Doc to Redeem the Rebel

For questions and comments about the quality of this book, please contact us at CustomerService@Harlequin.com.

Harlequin Enterprises ULC
22 Adelaide St. West, 41st Floor
Toronto, Ontario M5H 4E3, Canada
www.Harlequin.com

Printed in U.S.A.

Born and raised on the Wirral Peninsula in England, **Charlotte Hawkes** is mom to two intrepid boys who love her to play building block games with them and who object loudly to the amount of time she spends on the computer. When she isn't writing—or building with blocks—she is company director for a small Anglo/French construction firm. Charlotte loves to hear from readers, and you can contact her at her website: charlotte-hawkes.com.

Books by Charlotte Hawkes

Harlequin Medical Romance

Billionaire Twin Surgeons

Forbidden Nights with the Surgeon
Shock Baby for the Doctor

Royal Christmas at Seattle General

The Bodyguard's Christmas Proposal

Reunited on the Front Line

Second Chance with His Army Doc

The Doctor's One Night to Remember
Reunited with His Long-Lost Nurse
Tempted by Her Convenient Husband
His Cinderella Houseguest
Neurosurgeon, Single Dad...Husband?

Visit the Author Profile page
at Harlequin.com for more titles.

To my boys,
twelve years and ten years *already*—where have those years gone?

Congratulations on the M-thing, so incredibly proud of you both—make the most of it!

Mont, thanks for reading the first couple of chapters and enjoying them so much!

Means more than you can know.

$(xxx)^{n+1}$

Praise for
Charlotte Hawkes

"[The author's] research for this book is evident and lends a very authentic touch. With her talent, author Charlotte Hawkes could probably write in any sub-genre, but she brings this medical story to life."

—*Harlequin Junkie* on
Tempted by Her Convenient Husband

CHAPTER ONE

CONNOR MASON SLID his motorbike—an Italian super-sport racing motorcycle that was equal parts impressive and aggressive—to a razor-sharp halt in the layby and glowered down the valley to the chocolate-box-quaint houses below as they basked in summer's evening glow. This was the place at its best, the bucolic-looking villages of Upper Meadwood and Little Meadwood, and Connor's glower deepened.

He'd never really had much of an appetite for either place.

Gripping the handlebars of his bike white-knuckle-tight, he allowed his gaze to sweep from one side of the valley to the other. Rolling meadows swept down the south-west side, all dotted with cows and sheep, whilst a vast woodland still blanketed the north and east sides. Meadwood, where the meadow and woods met, and all held within the gentle embrace of two remaining arms of a freshwater river, which was the destination of eager fishermen all year round. Those picture-postcard houses with their pretty thatched roofs, hewn from local stone, all circled a village green that hosted everything from farmers' markets to national cross-country events, and from summer fetes to Christmas fairs.

And Connor loathed it all.

In the city you could slip by unnoticed. Anonymous. In a place like this, where everyone knew everyone else's business, it was impossible to do anything without the entire village having an opinion on the matter and voicing it. Loudly.

Not least the disdain many of them had felt at having the roustabout spawn of a drug-addled mother foisted on their peaceful little haven. He hadn't been that welcome the first time, and he'd been positively loathed the second time. Little wonder that he'd made his final escape a couple of months before his sixteenth birthday. If he could have left earlier, then he would have.

But he wasn't that angry, poverty-stricken, good-for-nothing kid any more. He didn't have to be here.

With a sharp kick, his obscenely expensive and even more obscenely well-tuned motorbike rumbled comfortingly into life as Connor held it motionless in the layby. Quietly reassuring him that with one acceleration, one spin, it could take him back away from this damned place with little more than a cloud of dust and a deep-throated roar and no one would ever know that he had come back.

But then…that would mean *Vivian* would never know that he had come back.

Vivian.

The foster mum who had been the closest person he'd ever had to a proper maternal figure—the only person. His biological mother wouldn't have even noticed whether he was there or not, had it not been for the fact that she could put her toddler son to work as a useful distraction whilst she stole more from whichever unsuspecting target had fallen into her path on any given day. Actually being loved, or cared about, had never factored into Connor's early life—until Vivian.

From the day he'd first been brought to her as a scrappy, dirty, malnourished six-year-old to the day his wicked excuse for a biological mother had tracked him down and snatched him back—and then again from the day he'd made Vivian his one phone call from that police station to the day he'd left her for that army assessment centre at fifteen years and ten months.

No matter what, Vivian had been the one person to always have his back. Unequivocally and vociferously. Taking no nonsense from anyone who had tried to say that she was wasting her time on a down-and-out kid like him.

Connor grinned suddenly—unexpectedly—at the memory of his foster mother. He remembered her as characteristically calm, caring and gentle, but when someone mistreated one of her foster kids… woe betide them!

As for her fierce independence…

Well! If that was why she hadn't told him about her declining health months ago—*years*, even—

then he was only grateful for the message that had reached him via his former army commander's widow, whose husband had once been one of Vivian's contacts for her fostering.

He owed her everything, and now she needed him. Which meant that turning around and leaving simply wasn't an option.

Dammit.

With that grim curse, Connor straightened up and rotated his hand inward to give the bike some throttle, and then began to pull out of the layby just as a loud rattling broke the silence, and a rusty pick-up truck appeared out of a hidden dip in front of him.

Hurtling up the narrow, winding country lane from the village, clearly on the wrong side of the road, the vehicle rattled worryingly as it lurched and bumped on the gravelly surface, bearing down on Connor far too fast. It was all he could do to throw all his body weight on one side in order to skid himself and his pride-and-joy motorbike into the safety of the ditch on the opposite side of the road as the truck flew by.

A few heart-stopping seconds later, the old truck careened off into the ditch on what would have been Connor's side of the road.

But there wasn't time to lie there. There wasn't even time for him to catch his breath. Scrambling to his feet, adrenalin still pumping through his veins, Connor threw off his crash helmet and vaulted out of the narrow channel, ignoring the screams of protest from his right thigh and arm. In the split second before the crash, he had caught sight of the elderly driver and now, with his surgeon instincts prickling the back of his neck, he couldn't shake the notion that something had been…*off.*

Connor raced back up the road and to the crashed pick-up truck, ignoring the way his stomach churned in horror.

The rear end was up out of the ditch with one wheel barely skimming the road, and the other clearly in the air, with most of the weight resting on the crumpled tin can of a bonnet. However, it was the stench of burning oil that assailed Connor's senses the most, clinging in the air and warning of a potential explosion.

Half jumping, half sliding into the ditch, he made for the driver's door and peered through the mud-caked window. It wasn't entirely a shock to see the grey-and-white-haired driver slumped unconscious against the steering wheel—if Connor's fleeting pre-crash memory was accurate, then the man had already been slumped over the wheel at the time of the accident—a heart attack, perhaps? Either way, the blood seeping out of a wound on his forehead and down to his equally grey beard was a concerning sight. Grasping the rusted handle of the pick-up's door, Connor yanked with all of his considerable might.

The metal creaked worryingly, but it refused to open, no match for the buckled vehicle's frame. A second heft yielded no better a result. Connor released the door for a moment to regroup. He could smash the glass, but that would mean raining shards down on his impromptu patient. Hardly ideal.

With a low curse, Connor launched himself over the bonnet and to the other side.

The angle of the car into the ditch meant that any effort to open this door was going to be just as futile, but at least smashing this window wouldn't risk harming the unconscious driver. Taking a deep breath and turning his head over one shoulder, Connor lifted his elbow and showered glass over the grass below him and the dirty, ripped passenger seat. A few seconds later, he was through the window and into the compact cab where a melee of aromas seemed to attack his olfactory senses.

First was the smell of alcohol that was somehow both fruity sweet and gut-wrenchingly sour, but, more concerningly, there was the pungent smell of leaking fuel.

He needed to get the old man out of there. Fast.

'Hey. *Hey!*' Connor shouted, hoping to rouse the man even as he lifted his fingers to check for a pulse, the adrenalin kicking harder at the incredibly weak beat. 'You awake?'

It wasn't a good sign that the man didn't even stir. From alcohol? Or from some medical emergency?

The lack of a seat belt certainly couldn't have helped the old man's chances, either. Though it might make it easier for Connor to move him now—

if he could figure out how to get his patient out of the vehicle.

Leaning back on the filthy seats, Connor carefully extended his good leg across the man's chest and kicked hard at the driver's door, shocked when it groaned but then gave way.

Crawling quickly back out of the passenger window, he raced around the truck and heaved the damaged door open the rest of the way before hauling the old guy out a foot. Then, keeping the old man's back to his own chest, and slipping his arms under his patient's armpits, Connor prepared to haul him all the way out.

'Wait. *Stop!*'

Connor lifted his head at the shout, just as a woman ran down the hill towards him.

And for a moment, he forgot where he was.

Dressed in running kit, with a longish, blondish ponytail swinging over her shoulders, she was certainly pretty, yet there should have been nothing so strikingly arresting about the woman to cause such an uncharacteristic, uninvited response. An instant attraction, but unlike any he'd experienced before. In Meadwood, of all places.

Well, there was no way he was letting *that* happen.

Irritated, Connor thrust the unwanted sensation out of the way, and instead turned his attention back to getting his patient away from the vehicle.

'Stay back,' he instructed, gritting his teeth as he

moved the deadweight of the old man a little further out of the seat. 'You need to call for an ambulance. Fire service, too.'

'Stop!' the woman shouted, a little louder this time as she waggled a phone before thrusting it in her back pocket. 'I already called them. Air ambulance is on its way. In the meantime, don't move him. He could have neck or back injuries.'

'I'm aware of that.'

'Then you shouldn't move him until I've assessed him.' She hurried over to within feet of him and he was abruptly struck by stunning blue eyes.

As vivid as the blue of the morpho butterfly that he'd seen on his travels through South America.

Where the heck had that thought come from?

He dragged himself back to the moment to find the woman had inserted herself into his rescue, her head bent to the old man.

'Excuse me…'

'Lester?' she said, ignoring him, concentrating instead on the patient. 'Lester, it's Nell, can you hear me?'

Lester?

The name scratched at something deep inside Connor's chest. In that black place where other, normal people had a heart.

Lester Jones? Old Farmer Jones? One of the villagers who had made Connor's childhood at Meadwood even harder than it had needed to be? The man who had spent the better part of a decade helping to spread one malicious rumour after another about the feral kid who Vivian Macey had had the poor sense to foster.

Connor had lost count of how many enemy combatants he'd saved over the past decade but he'd take any one of them over Lester-ruddy-Jones right now. Lucky for the farmer that the Hippocratic oath meant so much to him.

Gritting his teeth, Connor secured his grip even tighter on the old man.

'Stop!' The woman—Nell—glowered up at him. 'Can you just set him down for a moment?'

'Not really.' Connor didn't know why it took him such an effort to keep his voice even—he was usually renowned for his cool head under fire. 'Smell anything?'

'It isn't about whether Lester has been drinking or—'

'Not that; smell again,' he commanded quietly, even as he hauled Lester out a little further.

The woman—Nell—took a reluctant sniff before her eyes widened slightly.

'Diesel?'

'It's coming from the truck.' Connor nodded. 'With the damage to the engine, it could go up at any time. Hence why you should stay back.'

It would be bad enough for him or Lester to get caught in a fireball, he didn't need this innocent bystander getting injured too.

'Good call,' she muttered instead, paling slightly even as she held her ground.

Connor didn't know why that impressed him as much as it did.

'Just stay clear.'

'No.' She shook her head, moving to the truck door. 'You keep lifting and I'll grab Lester's legs as soon as his torso is free.'

His chest pulled tight.

'You need to get out of harm's way…'

'Not happening.'

The woman was positively infuriating.

'The truck could go up any moment.'

'Then the sooner you pull Lester free, the sooner we can get him secured and both get out of harm's way.'

And as much as he didn't like it, there was a steely quality to her tone that warned him that she was serious. But the quicker they achieved their objective, the better. His brain whirred.

'Fine. I think there was a tattered blanket in the footwell. If you can grab that, then perhaps we could use it as a bit of a makeshift stretcher.'

Nodding briskly, Nell obeyed. Moments later, she was back out with the ragged material spread out on the gravel above the ditch.

'Ready?' she asked.

'Lift on three,' he confirmed. 'One, two, lift.'

The pair worked together quickly and efficiently to free the unconscious man, moving him as far away from the truck as possible before assessing his injuries. The breathing wasn't as shallow as he might have feared, and his pulse was surprisingly strong.

Mean drunk or not, looking down at the unconscious man, Connor was glad that he nonetheless felt a sense of duty and responsibility. As a doctor he'd pledged an oath to help people—*all* people—including those who had made his already miserable childhood even more unpleasant. As a human being, it meant that the lessons Vivian had taught him hadn't been wasted.

He didn't care to imagine the hardened, cold human he would surely have become without the intervention of his foster mother. A brief moment of relief stabbed through him.

Returning to Meadwood might have been the last thing he'd ever wanted to do, but if Vivian had died before he'd had a chance to see her again, then he wasn't sure he'd have been able to live with himself.

'Breathing and pulse seem good, no broken bones or obvious injuries, and no indication of internal bleeding at this stage. Though I'd have preferred to stabilise him better before moving him to assess any further.'

'The air ambulance shouldn't be too long; the base is only about thirty miles away as the crow flies.'

And there was no reason for that to make him feel suddenly oddly nostalgic for the army life he'd only recently left behind, and the fellow soldiers he'd actually thought of as friends.

Then the moment passed as two deep blue pools turned to him and he told himself his insides couldn't possibly have just flip-flopped in some ridiculous way.

'Okay.' His gaze flickered between the old man and the wreck of the pick-up truck. The stench of fuel was now almost overpowering, and Connor felt an odd sense of foreboding. 'Maybe we should risk moving him a little further away.'

She followed his gaze, her lip caught in her teeth in a way he was sure he had no business noticing.

'You could be right.'

Taking each end of the blanket and trying to keep it as taut as they could, the pair moved their patient another twenty metres or so down the road, closer to where Connor's bike was still lodged in its own ditch. They had barely set Lester back down when there was a loud explosion, and a burst of flames shot up from the wrecked pick-up.

'Your second good call in the space of ten minutes,' Nell muttered calmly, though her white face betrayed her shock.

'We need to keep Lester stable until the helicopter arrives.' He dismissed the compliment. 'There's an emergency medical bag in my motorbike top box. Can you grab it?'

Nell nodded, and as he tossed her the keys he got the impression that she was glad of the distraction.

'I can't believe he isn't worse than he is,' she called over her shoulder. 'I'd thought maybe a broken rib, maybe even a pneumothorax, given the size of that old steering wheel, but you didn't find anything?'

'Nothing apparent,' Connor confirmed.

Then again, if he was right that the old man had already been half passed-out before the accident—arguably due to alcohol—then his body might not have been braced for impact and so he might have managed to avoid the usual type of RTC injuries.

Not that he was about to say any of that to Nell. She clearly knew and seemed to like Lester, so he wasn't about to set her against him before he'd had a chance to tell the police his side of events. It was almost a relief when she returned with the medical bag.

'Thanks. Okay, we should start by stabilising his head and neck,' Connor determined, delving into the bag. 'Then we can do a more thorough check-over. Can you hold his head steady whilst I put this on?'

For the next twenty minutes or so, they worked together surprisingly seamlessly as they attended to Lester's injuries, using the equipment from Connor's emergency medical kit. Connor found himself uncharacteristically stealing glances at Nell as he admired her calm, collected demeanour, which matched his own so well. By the time the air ambulance touched down in the field next to them he was confident that their patient was as comfortable as he could be.

'Connor Mason, trauma surgeon,' Connor introduced himself briefly to the paramedic who reached him first. 'Patient is a male, late sixties, approximately half an hour ago he drove off the road at around thirty miles per hour, and crashed into the ditch over there but he was already unconscious moments before the accident.'

'How can you be sure?'

It wasn't a challenge, merely fact-checking.

'He nearly collided with me,' Connor explained. 'I just about managed to get my motorbike out of his path but he was no more than two metres away when I saw him through the windscreen.'

'Right.' The paramedic nodded, clearly taking in all the information.

'I managed to reach him within a minute after the crash, and he was still totally unresponsive. He hasn't regained consciousness since, but BP is a little elevated. However, there's a strong smell of alcohol both on his breath and in the vehicle, so you might want to include that in your initial assessment since heavy alcohol consumption is known to diminish baroreceptor sensitivity.'

'He has a laceration to his right temple, and a possible head injury hasn't been ruled out,' Nell added.

'I take it that he wasn't thrown from the vehicle, then?' the paramedic asked, kneeling down beside the older man to begin a preliminary assessment of his own. 'You moved him here?'

Connor sensed, rather than saw, Nell nod and open her mouth to speak but he wasn't about to let her take any blame for moving the patient.

'That was my call,' he interjected. 'I could smell diesel leaking from the vehicle and I felt it safer to move the patient rather than risk him being inside when the explosion happened.'

'We both deemed it safer to do so,' Nell added firmly, evidently not wanting him to protect her.

The paramedic nodded, taking in all the information, and beginning to relay it to the doctor who was already hurrying over. Still, Connor held his position until a hand touched his arm gently.

'Let them take over,' Nell murmured. 'You're clearly a great doctor but he's their patient now.'

'Yeah, but—'

'They have all the equipment, too,' she cut him off softly.

Reluctantly, Connor bit back any further objection. Whether he liked it or not, she had a point. Forcing himself to take a step back, he watched the crew complete the same assessment that he had, and then be able to check further. Ultimately, however, they confirmed Lester was stable enough to move and began loading him onto a stretcher and into the helicopter.

'Not accustomed to being on the sidelines, are

you?' that voice asked quietly. Almost empathetically.

'I prefer being busy,' he heard himself admit, wondering what it had been that had made him answer this relative stranger, when he usually didn't reveal much about himself, even to colleagues.

Finally, Connor watched as the bird lifted off, its rotors thrumming powerfully, and felt a strange wave of disappointment that—aside from the less-than-desirable circumstances—his time with the unexpectedly captivating Nell was at an end.

Though perhaps that was a good thing, since he was all too aware of her beside him, brushing against his arm as she turned, and exhaling a long, deep breath.

'Well, that wasn't exactly the Saturday afternoon that I'd anticipated. Doubt it was yours either.'

That might have been the understatement of the century.

'Not exactly,' he agreed grimly, and then before he could stop the words from tumbling unbidden from his mouth, he heard himself ask, 'Can I buy you a drink?'

He wasn't sure which of them was more surprised.

'I...can't,' she answered regretfully after a moment. 'I was supposed to be somewhere about half an hour ago. I have to go.'

'I understand.' He forced a bright smile though he couldn't explain what it was that made him wish she would delay her plans a little longer. 'Well, I should see if my ride has fared any better than Lester's pick-up truck.'

Still he didn't move.

Why was he wishing he could find a reason to stay and talk to her some more? Properly.

Whatever that meant.

He was hardly known for his love of conversation. After all, why use fifty words when a handful would suffice? Yet in this instant, he would happily have spent the evening sitting across a table from her, in some quiet country pub, learning all about this one particular woman.

Ridiculous.

He stuffed the curious notion back down and resolutely made his way back up the road to where his prized machine was still languishing in the ditch, trying not to notice how fluid it seemed when Nell fell silently into step beside him. This...*peculiarity* he felt had to just be about the strangeness of being back in this place, after all these years.

They walked together in companionable silence until they reached his crash site. Surprisingly, aside from a few dings to the usually polished paintwork, it looked as though it had come through the ordeal relatively unscathed.

Which was more than could be said for himself.

And he didn't just mean the burning sensation in his right arm and down the side of his torso.

'Right,' Connor announced, manoeuvring the

heavy motorcycle upright and out of the ditch before retrieving his crash helmet. 'I'd offer you a lift but… I don't have a second crash helmet on me.'

Plus, he'd never offered anyone a ride on his motorbike. *Never.* The bike had always been his, and his alone.

'It's fine,' Nell confirmed, shifting her weight from one foot to the other without leaving.

He wondered if perhaps she was reconsidering the idea of getting a drink.

Wondered, or hoped?

'Well, thanks again for your help with Lester,' he told her, hoping to break the awkwardness. 'And for letting me use your medical kit.'

'Of course.' She nodded, still hesitating. As though there was something else she wanted to say but was holding back. 'And now you're heading…?'

He could feel the shutters coming down inside him. Familiar. And usually welcome.

But now…? He couldn't quite explain this odd sensation firing him up inside. As if *she* was the one causing the blood in his veins to effervesce.

But an attraction was the last thing he needed. This visit was about paying his respects to Vivian; it wasn't about getting to know some stranger.

'I'll just stay here a while,' he told her. Coldly.

'Right. Well… I'll leave you to it.'

One last pause and then she was gone, jogging down the hill in the same direction as the one Connor was headed. Hardly surprising, of course, since the road only led into the Meadwood valley or out of it. Still, Connor found himself pretending that he didn't lament the loss of her company.

At all.

Nor the evaporation of that inexplicable...*something* that appeared to have set all sorts of thoughts tumbling through his head—none of which he was ready to identify yet.

And still, as he faltered there on his bike and glowered accusingly down the valley, he couldn't seem to stop the thoughts altogether.

Like the fact that he couldn't remember a time he had felt such a strong spark of attraction, but that it should happen here, of all places, was particularly galling.

Another reason to hate this place.

He could pretend that it was because he'd never been built to appreciate the countryside—it was too dull, too uneventful, the exact opposite of the life he'd ultimately craved for himself.

He was a thrill-seeker, a risk-taker, and, more than that, he was a man who had always loved a challenge.

But it was more than just the location.

As pretty as it was, as far as Connor was concerned the quaint, chocolate-box Little Meadwood was all a façade. A mere veil shrouding people who had never really made him feel as if he was one of them. Take an old soak whose own sins were carefully overlooked simply because he'd been born and bred in the village, whilst newcomers like him—even an innocent six-year-old who had simply had a shamefully bad start to life—would always be viewed with suspicion, and distrust.

And Upper Meadwood—lorded over by Lord Percival and his family—was even worse.

Without warning, something flickered deep, deep within him, and Connor was startled to realise that the hurt and resentment that he'd thought he'd long since buried were still simmering somewhere inside.

Or maybe it's more like fear.

The voice whispered in his head—almost startling him.

Maybe you're just afraid that coming back here is too much a reminder of the angry, lost kid that you once were?

Swiftly, Connor slammed the uninvited thoughts away—but it was too late. Like it or not, that voice held more than a grain of truth. When he'd turned his back on the village almost twenty years ago to join the army, he'd sworn to himself that he would never, *never* return.

And by God, he'd remained true to his word.

He'd toured the world, from Cyprus to Belize, and from Iraq to the USA—relishing the fact that he never stayed in the same place for too long. He'd lived the life of ten other men. Maybe a hundred. And he'd put his bitter, grimy childhood firmly in the past where it belonged.

Until now.

And until the unexpected phone call that had him feeling adrift. Lost. Struggling to come to terms with the idea that this unparalleled woman might not be for this world much longer.

It seemed so…*wrong*.

So now, here he was. Back in Little Meadwood after all.

Something bowled around in his chest, though he pretended he didn't notice. He'd get in, get out, and be back to his proper life.

Connor revved his engine, the sound echoing through the valley as he skidded out some shale, taking off down the hill towards the village. Adrenalin pumped as he inhaled the mixture of hot, oily engine, tyres burning on the asphalt, and the freshly mown grass of a nearby field, and then he hurtled skilfully through the narrow, winding roads.

And hoped that he wasn't racing back into the hellfire that was his past.

CHAPTER TWO

AROUND VIVIAN'S LITTLE COTTAGE, Nell was faffing.

There was no getting away from it.

She'd been edgy ever since her encounter with the deliciously sinful Connor Mason on the road into the village, and no amount of heroic stories on Vivian's part—or their foster mother's proudly shared blurry photos—could possibly have prepared Nell for the impact of meeting the man in the flesh.

The man defied all belief, and surely no picture could have adequately captured how impossibly broad-shouldered, how ridiculously chisel-featured, how outrageously masculine he was. Enough to make her blush just thinking about him.

Stop it!

Setting down one of the few knick-knacks Vivian had, Nell forced herself to back away from the side table as she pressed her free hand to her chest. As though that might somehow rein in her racing heart.

What on earth was the matter with her? She never acted like this—as if there was something wholly carnal lurking inside her that had never once shown itself to her before, in all her thirty-three years.

Yet how else was she supposed to justify her body's almost visceral reaction to Connor Mason, out there at the crash site? How else could she explain why—as dedicated to her career as she usually prided herself on being—despite the circumstances of their encounter when she should surely have been solely focused on the injured Lester, she'd found herself noticing all kinds of things about the man whose very presence seemed to make the air around him crackle with thrilling electricity?

And Lord—what about that understated strength and power he'd exuded? More potent than any cologne.

Her heart gave another crazy lurch in her chest as another delicious image bounced around her head.

It certainly hadn't hurt that his motorbike leathers had hugged his powerful thighs like a second skin. Or that his short hair had been slightly tousled from his crash helmet.

And it didn't matter how fiercely she chided herself for such wayward thoughts, nor how carefully she pointed out to herself that the last thing she should want was to be attracted to some hot, biker bad-boy who—once he'd done his duty seeing Vivian—would likely roar out of their village as quickly as he'd roared into it.

Yet, she couldn't seem to shake the effects of their chance encounter.

Despite her having been back home for over an hour now, her nerves were even more frayed than before. It didn't help that every time she could have sworn that she heard a growling engine she found herself peeking out of the living room window and half expecting to see him race past, revving the kind of motorbike that she usually hated, but that seemed to match him so seamlessly.

There was something about the man that had seemed to draw her in, and so now here she was—*faffing.*

Aside from the knick-knacks, she'd fussed with the cushions on Vivian's armchairs, straightening them for the hundredth time that hour. She'd clicked on the kettle on the worktop at least five times yet each time she'd forgotten to actually make a drink. She'd even adjusted the picture frames on the wall, making sure that they hung straight and true.

Nell sighed heavily. Clearly, she was being ridiculous, but she couldn't seem to stop. She'd felt…odd. Unsettled. So unlike herself.

And it hadn't been because of the circumstances of Lester's accident—although treating a patient right there in the field, rather than having them brought into her in A & E was certainly a very different experience—it had been about Connor himself.

Was it the way he looked, with sharp jawline, smoky-grey eyes, and to-die-for body? Or perhaps the way he carried himself, with an air of both danger and confidence woven so tightly together? Maybe it was the stories she'd heard about him over the past twenty years—almost folklore around Little

Meadwood—combined with the shock of actually meeting him for the first time ever?

Whatever it was, the effect had been so much, and so fast, that even now it was almost dizzying. A rush that went straight through her body and right up to her head. Like a large hit of ristretto after a year-long abstinence from coffee. But she was being utterly ridiculous if she actually believed a man like Connor would ever look at someone like her—even if she had wanted him to, which she certainly did *not*—since the man was clearly everything she wasn't: confident, daring, and unapologetically sexy.

Pacing the living room, she stopped by the bureau to straighten the photos on there, her hands automatically reaching for the one of a sixteen-year-old Connor in his military uniform, taken the last time he'd ever been back to Little Meadwood—months before she herself had arrived at Vivian's as a recently orphaned thirteen-year-old.

But, even if she'd never met him, Connor had never been a complete stranger to her given how she'd followed his progress over the past twenty years through Vivian.

The older woman's love and pride was evident for all of her many charges, but perhaps few more so than the boy who had essentially been like a son to her for nine years. Photos were proudly hung all over the tiny cottage of all Vivian's longer-term charges over the decades—including one of herself when she'd graduated as a doctor—and it was good for a foster child to see just how much they meant to the endlessly caring and patient Vivian.

Everyone in Meadwood—and no doubt several villages beyond—had been proudly told how well her former charges were doing, and Connor Mason was no exception. A career-driven, dedicated trauma surgeon who had travelled the world and learned his craft within various theatres of war. Nell knew the stories almost off by heart.

Even so, seeing him in action today—seeing the way he moved with purpose and precision whilst saving mean old Lester Jones's life—made something in her shift, in a way that she couldn't explain.

There was something magnetic about him. Maybe it was his broad shoulders, or his piercing grey eyes that seemed to stop her heart from beating in her very chest. Or maybe it was the way he had rushed into that life-threatening emergency, completely fearless and focused, taking charge of the situation without hesitation.

Or perhaps it was the way he had looked at her, with a hint of curiosity and something else that she couldn't quite identify in those gunmetal depths, that made her feel fluttery and a little light-headed. Like a swooning schoolkid rather than a grown woman.

She should hate herself for it. Instead, she found it strangely thrilling.

Boy, was she in trouble.

Nell shook her head, trying to clear her thoughts. She needed to focus on Vivian, not on some mysterious and attractive stranger. She took a deep breath, reminding herself of the reason she was here—to take care of Vivian, just as Vivian had taken care of her all those years ago.

But as she went to the kitchen to finally make herself and her foster mum a cup of tea, she couldn't help but feel a sense of anticipation that stubbornly remained even when she chided herself that Connor was clearly back for Vivian, not to meet or spend time with herself or any other of his fellow foster kids.

So why, when she carried the steaming mugs of tea into the living room and called Vivian down from upstairs, did she sneak a glance in the hallway mirror to take in the flushed cheeks and the strange excitement in the eyes of the woman in her reflection?

As though there was something about her encounter with Connor today that had her feeling alive in a way she hadn't felt for a long time.

Maybe ever.

It made no sense, yet by the time the doorbell rang for the other visitors she knew Vivian was expecting that evening, it was all Nell could do not to leap out of her chair like the proverbially scalded cat.

Her heart hammered so loudly as she moved down the hallway to open the door that she was shocked her eagle-eyed and bat-eared foster mother couldn't hear it—that the entire village couldn't hear it. And when she opened the door to find Ruby and Ivan, two of Vivian's other former long-term charges, standing on the doorstep, Nell tried to tell herself that any sense of disappointment she felt that they weren't Connor was purely on Vivian's behalf. Certainly not because she herself was eager to see him again.

And then she hastily set down the already spotless photo of a teenage Connor in military uniform, which she didn't realise she'd picked up to dust.

Connor hadn't been able to stop the sense of unease that had washed over him even as his motorbike had crossed the single-lane humpback bridge into Little Meadwood. So much so that he'd carried on straight through the village to the old toll bridge on the other side, and back out of the valley and into the next county. Then, when he'd forced himself to turn around again, he'd driven straight through it and back to the city. Third time was—as the saying went—a charm.

Not that it felt much like a charm.

He might want to see Vivian but still couldn't reconcile being back in this place.

Not even if it gives you another chance to talk to the woman from earlier?

Too late, he silenced the needling voice in his head.

He was just here to see his foster mother. In. Out. No harm, no foul. Easy.

But as he pulled up to the small cottage on the outskirts of Little Meadwood, he felt a surge of memories flood back.

The home looked just as he remembered it. Small and quaint with the ubiquitous thatched roof and painted timber window frames.

Vivian's beautiful garden was as awash with colourful flowers as it had ever been and it was like stepping back in time. For a moment, Connor forgot why he was there, then he took a deep breath and got off his bike and removed his helmet and gloves, his boots crunching on the gravel path as he made his way towards the front door, a painted stone winking up at him from the side of the path, making him stop abruptly.

How had he forgotten about the tiny stone frog family? Vivian had encouraged each foster child to choose and paint their own stone—a green frog, a yellow frog, a blue-and-red frog, it didn't matter—and then they added it somewhere in the front garden. Her idea had been that every one of her foster kids would know that they were remembered by her; but also that kids who really needed it—kids like him—could hold onto the idea that they were a part of some kind of family, somewhere.

Of course he'd resisted at first, choosing to paint a black-and-orange poison dart frog—his way of warning others to stay away. In response, Vivian had painted a bromeliad on another stone and set it down next to his, and then she'd taught him about the symbiotic relationship between the two. It was the first time he'd actually felt *heard*. By anybody.

It was strange to be back here, in this place that was the closest thing to a home that he'd ever known. Pausing for a moment by the alliums as the scent unexpectedly assailed his brain as much as his nostrils, Connor was unprepared for the memories that suddenly dislodged themselves and dropped into the periphery of his mind. Memories that he hadn't even known he'd made, and which he couldn't quite grasp even now. But far from the hollower echoes that he'd replayed all these years, these new, hazy recollections gave the impression they were of happier moments. Or, if not actually *happier*, then at least snatched moments that had been less miserable.

He paused a moment longer, waiting to see if they would become any clearer, but instead they remained stubbornly out of view.

Perhaps he'd imagined it.

Shaking his head as if to dislodge the nonsensical ideas, Connor took another couple of steps forward towards the house but then another scent hit him. Harder this time. And, as if on autopilot, Connor reached over the wall and selected a few plump, juicy blackberries from the neighbour's tempting blackberry bush that had always been there. How many times had he been yelled at by Old Man Luddlington for stealing his blackberries, or his apples?

Strange to realise the old man would be long gone by now. Almost…sad?

Popping the blackberries in his mouth—as mouth-watering as they'd always been—Connor took a moment to savour the taste, shocked when another memory crept inside his head. Again of Vivian, and the first time she had taken him blackberry picking in the hedges by the farmers' fields, and then showed him how she made her famous blackberry jam. The wave of nostalgia slammed into him hard, almost knocking him over.

It was one thing knowing logically all that his foster mother had done for him. But it was quite another reliving it in such vivid detail after all this time.

She'd taught him more about nature in that one afternoon than anyone else had ever taught him in his life until that moment. It was the afternoon he'd discovered his love for foraging and wilderness training that had led him to take survival courses, and ultimately realise that the military was where his path lay.

She'd probably saved his life that day. Without her, his free time would doubtless have been spent in increasingly more criminal pursuits rather than building dens and wild food harvesting.

Maybe if she wasn't too sick yet he could talk her into joining him in the kitchen so that the two of them could whip up a batch of that special jam together? It might be the better part of two decades since he'd last made it, but he figured he could still remember how.

Strangely buoyed, Connor strode down the remainder of the garden path and knocked confidently on the front door. But when the door swung open seconds later only for a familiar face to stare back at him, it felt as if he'd just been punched squarely in the chest.

It took him a moment to realise that the blow that seemed to have knocked every last bit of air from his lungs wasn't physical. Then another moment to try to regain enough of that air to breathe.

'You?' He barely recognised his own voice.

But it was too late to walk away now.

'Nell,' she prompted tightly. As though she thought he'd already forgotten her name.

He hadn't.

He couldn't have even if he'd wanted to. Though the effect she had on him made no sense.

Connor tried to give himself another mental shake. It wasn't as though he hadn't experienced instant attraction before—he might have spent his adult life avoiding romantic entanglements but he wasn't exactly a monk—yet this was more than just lust. More than mere chemistry.

Now that the emergency with Lester was no longer taking his focus, there was nothing to distract him from experiencing the full pull of this woman.

And the sensations she sent coursing through him were far more volatile; explosive, even. So irrational that he couldn't even think straight, let alone speak straight.

And he hated himself for his lack of control.

'I'm here,' he managed to grit out, 'to see Vivian.'

Because—as if he needed to remind himself again—his foster mother was who he'd come back to Little Meadwood for. Not to go off indulging in some unwanted enthralment with her carer—or whoever Nell was.

Of all the times to be attracted to someone, this had to be the most inappropriate.

And the most unacceptable.

He commanded himself to pull his head together.

Yet still that peculiar punch of enthralment vibrated painfully somewhere inside his chest as his gaze drank in the woman in front of him.

Now out of her running gear, she wore an electric-blue V-neck T-shirt that clung to feminine curves—no less mouth-watering for their subtlety—and only intensified the hue of her expressive eyes that right now were less morpho-butterfly-blue and more the same forget-me-not-blue as some of the flowers he'd just been admiring. Even so, they were as captivating and vibrant as a few hours earlier.

More so, perhaps.

Out of the brighter daylight, her hair seemed more honeyed, but her skin was every bit as silky smooth as before. If he reached out, would it feel just as soft? His palms actually itched at the thought of finding out.

At his sides, Connor balled them into fists and shoved them into the pockets of his leather jacket, trying valiantly to keep his eyes from wandering to Nell's sinfully inviting mouth with the pale pink lips that had seemed bare this afternoon, but now had a hint of a sheen, making his mouth water every bit as much as the berries had done only seconds before.

He suspected that if he kissed her, she would taste even better than they had.

What the heck was wrong with him?

Connor dragged his head back to reality. Or tried to. But how was it that he was suddenly so much more aware of the evening breeze as it moved around him? Licking at his skin.

Making him feel…

Suddenly, a couple of kids shrieked from the playground down on the green and both he and Nell jerked their heads to watch.

Something and nothing—but at least now it gave him a beat to regroup.

Whatever his attraction to this woman, it was wholly inappropriate. And he refused to allow it to take root.

The woman must be here to care for his foster mother, and therefore he needed her focus to be entirely on her patient—with no distractions. Although, to be fair, from her actions with their impromptu patient earlier, he was already under the impression that her patients were always her primary focus regardless of a situation. Just as his were.

Which, unfortunately, only made him all the more attracted to her.

Still, stuffing down the unsolicited thoughts, Connor pasted a polite smile on his lips and thrust out his hand to Nell.

'It seems we meet again. Perhaps I should introduce myself properly this time. I'm Connor Mason, one of Vivian's former foster kids, and I'm guessing you, Nell, are Vivian's doctor?'

'I know who you are.'

Nell stared up at the newcomer, fighting to keep the dismay from showing on her face. At least, she told herself that it was *dismay* that she was feeling in that moment.

Certainly nothing else.

It definitely wasn't *awareness* sizzling through her at being confronted by all that startling…*maleness*…all over again—and this time right on her doorstep. Well… Vivian's doorstep.

It had been one thing working alongside the guy when she'd had the distraction of Lester and the accident, but now there was nothing else to focus her attention on besides the man standing right in front of her. Almost too close for comfort. His six-foot-two frame—or six-foot-three, maybe—filled up the narrow doorway of the cottage, with shoulders so deliciously broad and strong that they blocked out the rest of the warm, summer light. In all the years she'd spent with this cottage being her home, she couldn't recall it ever having been graced in such a way. As if it had shrunk a couple of sizes in the rain and was now too compact for a man like this. As though it might burst at the seams just from trying to contain him.

She couldn't even imagine him having grown up here—having actually lived here, in this cottage, in the same place that she had—all those decades ago.

He just seemed so...*out of place* for a village like Little Meadwood. A sleek, jagged, thrilling shape that was too restless to slot into such a soft, sleepy, laid-back jigsaw like this.

And yet she knew he had spent years as one of Vivian's first foster kids. For something like a decade?

How many times had she stared at the photos in Vivian's album, or listened to his name included in the 'absent friends' toast at the village Christmas Fair, and wondered what this man—this war hero—might actually be like in person?

Now, however, she found herself thinking that it was just as well that Connor hadn't returned before now. And not because she was finding it so disconcerting the way her very core seemed to crackle with sheer chemistry at the feel of all that heat emanating from his body; nor because the vague scent of his leathers was making her nerves jangle with all that *maleness.*

It shouldn't be such a struggle to get control of herself.

'I'm not Vivian's doctor,' she answered at length, somehow—*somehow*—managing to step aside far enough to allow him entry, though he had to duck under the cottage's low doorframe.

'Oh?'

With such a dark look he didn't need words to ask her what she was doing here.

Bizarrely, despite her reputation for being calm and unflappable whether she was facing a yelling patient or a terrified relative, Nell found herself reacting. Bristling. Allowing this man—this relative stranger—to get under her skin.

'Given that you've been away for the better part of two decades—' she tried to keep her voice even, nonetheless '—I'm not sure you have the right to waltz in here and demand to know precisely who everyone is and what they're doing here.'

His dark look turned to one of amusement.

'I didn't ask who everyone is,' he pointed out. 'I merely asked who *you* are.'

It was hardly an unreasonable question. So why was she reacting as she was? So out of character.

'For your information—' Nell fought to regroup '—I was also one of Vivian's foster kids.'

'Is that so?'

His voice was level but she knew she hadn't

imagined the look of surprise flashing across his features.

'From when I was thirteen to when I turned eighteen,' she heard herself continuing. As if she owed him an explanation. 'I arrived a few months after you'd left, though Vivian used to mention you regularly.'

His look darkened again.

'So you knew who I was on the road, earlier?'

'Not immediately.' She hesitated. Apparently she'd said something wrong, though she wasn't quite sure what that had been. 'I was more preoccupied with Lester.' Which wasn't exactly a lie. Just perhaps not the whole truth. 'I realised who you were afterwards.'

He grunted, but didn't answer. She drew in a breath, trying to reset her professional head.

'Look, Vivian took a late nap but she'll be down any moment. Do you want to just go through to the living room?'

She gestured down the narrow hallway, grateful that he went without argument. For a moment a part of her had feared he might turn around, fling one of those muscled legs over that powerful machine on the road, and roar off again.

Then she closed the door with deliberate care before taking a deep breath and following him down the narrow hallway.

'I should introduce Ruby,' she began, just before

he turned into the room. 'And Ivan. Both were also former charges of Vivian.'

He stopped so abruptly that Nell almost ran into the back of him. She opened her mouth to speak, then stopped, noting the odd expressions on the two men's faces. Her heart hammered for a split second as she realised that it might have been a mistake to have two Alpha males in such a cramped space. But then they each gave a gruff, almost incredulous laugh.

'Ivan?'

'Connor?'

As the men stepped towards each other as though to shake hands, only to instantly turn it into a wide bear hug, Nell glanced at Ruby. Her friend looked even more shocked than she herself felt.

'How long has it been?' Ivan growled, with an unexpected crack of emotion.

'Too long,' Connor's voice rumbled, and Nell wished she knew him well enough to understand what he was thinking in that moment. 'Decades.'

And then they lapsed into a silence that somehow seemed to make the air crackle.

'I'd forgotten that you two had known each other,' Nell confessed, when she couldn't stand the tension any longer. 'But I'd never realised that you'd been so close.'

The two men eyed each other somewhat wryly. A whole shared history passing between them in that one look.

'You could call it that,' Connor confirmed gruffly.

'What does that mean?' Nell and Ruby chorused. It seemed they were both as curious as each other, but the beat of silence didn't help.

'It means that if any of the local kids started beating on one of us then the other would have his back…' Connor offered simply in the end.

'And that was good enough,' Ivan finished just as simply.

Clearly that was all either of them was going to say.

'Right,' Nell offered flatly, trying not to let her mind race.

'Okay.' Ruby nodded, sounding equally bemused.

But they both knew only too well how fragile things were when you were a foster kid. And how hard it could be to feel truly at ease around others. It seemed they weren't about to press either of the men now. Even so, Nell found it harder to bite her tongue than it should have been—certainly harder than it had ever been with anyone else. She suddenly found that she wanted to know more about Connor. Wanted to know everything.

She was more than a little relieved when she heard Vivian begin to make her way downstairs, and all four of them leapt instinctively to help her. Ultimately, as the one closest to the door, it was Nell who won the honour.

'You've got a full house tonight,' she murmured quietly to her old foster mum, who squeezed her arm tightly as they made their way slowly down the hall.

'Is that so?' Vivian wheezed cheerfully. 'What did I do to deserve such wonderful kids like you lot?'

'Everything.' Nell made herself chuckle, but it was harder than it should be to speak past the lump in her throat.

Her foster mother had always been so strong, so full of life, and even fuller with love. To see her so frail now was like a kick in the teeth. And Nell knew the others felt exactly the same.

A moment later and the two of them were making their way through the door and to Vivian's chair. But she might have known the determined woman wouldn't allow herself to be settled down so easily.

'Well, if it isn't my favourite foster kids,' she rasped in delight, stepping forward to hug Ruby, then Ivan.

'You always say that to all of us,' Ivan rumbled in amusement as he enveloped her in his arms.

Nell's chest pulled tight at the way his powerful figure only highlighted Vivian's diminishing form. Not that Vivian would let that easily daunt her.

'Doesn't make it any less true,' she told him firmly. 'Just means I am truly blessed.'

Finally, she turned to the figure behind the door—the one she must have clocked out of the corner of her eye, but hadn't quite appreciated his identity until that moment.

'Connor,' she breathed, her voice rattling with emotion.

'Hey, Vivian.' Connor seemed to hesitate only for a moment before leaning down to wrap his muscled arms around her. Making her seem even more fragile than ever.

Nell couldn't help wondering how strange it might feel for him, being back in this place after all these years. Their foster mum had never said as much, yet Nell had always got the sense that Vivian had felt as though joining the army had been Connor's way of running away. From Meadwood, but also perhaps from his life.

Nell had always felt as though his departure had made Vivian sad, and a little disappointed—as though she'd felt she'd somehow failed him. But now, watching him hug the older woman, it appeared to Nell as though a sense of peace had begun to wash over both of them.

And she could certainly understand how that might be true.

For all that all of their circumstances might have been different—hers, Connor's, even Ivan's and Ruby's—the troubles and hardships any foster kids experienced could be similar. And through all the upheavals and changes, Vivian had always been there for them. Even if they'd had nothing else, she had been the one constant in their lives, a source of light.

Nell watched as Connor slowly—and, it seemed,

reluctantly—pulled back as he scanned Vivian's face. What did he make of the lines etched into her once smooth skin—those telltale signs of the illness that was slowly taking her away?

Nell's chest tightened painfully at the thought and she fought to swallow the beastly lump in her throat. She was grateful when Vivian finally broke the thick silence.

'You look good, kid.' Her voice was still raspy but filled with her characteristic love.

'You look like you're holding up pretty well too,' Connor replied with a smile that Nell just knew was his attempt to mask his sadness at the sight of her fading away.

She wasn't surprised when Vivian gave a weak snort of laughter.

'You never were a good liar—at least, not to me. Well, I might be stuck in this chair most of the time, but there's still a little life left in the old dog.'

Again, Nell found herself drawn to the way Connor's throat constricted, as well as the little tic in his tightening jaw that betrayed the fact that he was fighting to keep his emotions in check.

The way they all were right now. None of them could bear losing Vivian.

It was heartening, in a way, how many visitors she had enjoyed these past few months. Mostly former foster kids—and all of them demonstrating just what an incredible impact this one woman had had on so many lives.

Vivian Macey—foster mother and superwoman. Vivian was the reason why she and Ruby had never really left Meadwood. And why Ivan and a few others had each returned this week and declared their individual intentions to stick around, or at least visit more, for however long they were needed.

Did Connor intend to stay indefinitely, too? Or would he leave as abruptly as he had arrived? She couldn't answer that, yet she couldn't help hoping he would stay.

For Vivian, of course. She had no vested interest in what he did.

None at all.

Still, as the group settled down to chat, Nell found her gaze seeking him out despite herself. Assessing him. Trying to read his thoughts. And, inexplicably, trying not to let her mind wander into less acceptable territory.

Connor Mason was clearly a man accustomed to commanding attention and respect—that much had been clear from their encounter on the road with Lester—yet there was also something far more primal about him.

Something that made her mind keep wondering what it might be like to run her hands through his thick dark hair, to feel the strength of his broad shoulders against her fingertips.

She shook her head as though that might dispel both the heat from her cheeks and the unsolicited thoughts from her head, but even if that scattered the images for a moment, they crept back in all too quickly.

Since when did she indulge in such hormonal fantasies?

Jerking abruptly to her feet, she muttered some excuse about making tea and lurched around the crowded furniture, almost relieved that everyone else seemed too caught up in their conversations to hear her. Vivian was catching up on Connor's past few years, whilst Ruby and Ivan seemed to be having their own quiet, oddly intense conversation. There was no reason for her to feel this strange, pushed-out feeling. It made no sense.

Maybe she needed a bit of air.

Her head buzzing, Nell padded through to the kitchen and busied herself tidying up plates that were already neat, and wiping down counters that were already clean. And still, her thoughts crept off on a journey of their own.

In the other room, she could hear the sound of their laughter, and the occasional catch in Vivian's voice, and Connor's kindness and compassion with their foster mother was evident. Nell stared out of the window thoughtfully. Of course, she and Ruby had never really left Little Meadwood, and Ivan—despite being a busy surgeon—had always visited at least once a year. But in twenty years, Connor had never returned—although Nell was aware that, every few years, he had flown Vivian out to wherever he was working around the world, just for a break and so the two of them could catch up.

It had never made her feel quite so…envious before.

Filling the kettle, she absently set out the mugs and Vivian's favourite cup and saucer.

What was it about Connor Mason that was so unsettling? Was it really because a part of her feared that he was trying to swoop in and take control?

Or was there another reason why this one particular man affected her so strangely? Like it or not—and she did *not* like it, she told herself firmly—he seemed to have a crazy way of getting under her skin as no one else ever had before. Not even Jonathon.

Which is all the more reason for you to get a grip.

Nell began to pour the boiling water over the teabags, still schooling herself, when she heard the sound of footsteps behind her. The finest hairs prickled on her neck even before she turned to see Connor standing in the doorway, his watchful grey eyes raking over her and making her skin physically tingle.

And despite her stern warnings to herself it made it impossible to suppress the frisson of excitement that shot through her at such a gaze, pinning her to the spot and stealing every last bit of air from her lungs.

CHAPTER THREE

'CAN I HELP?'

Nell jerked her head up. It was such a mundane question yet it caused such a visceral reaction in her that it was almost laughable. And she probably *would* have laughed if only she'd been able to breathe. Instead, she simply stared back at him, hoping she didn't look as foolish or as jacked-up as she felt.

'Everything okay?' Connor's impossibly handsome frown skewered her all the more.

'Everything's great,' she answered, perhaps a little too quickly as her breath came back to her in a rush. 'No problems here. You get back to Vivian.'

'Actually, that's partly why I came in. I wanted to ask about how she's really doing.'

'You mean when she isn't pretending she's completely fine?' A wry smile tugged at the corners of Nell's mouth, the tea-making momentarily forgotten.

'Clearly I believed her these past few years when she told me it wasn't that bad,' he admitted. 'I should have returned earlier.'

Though Nell got the sense that he would rather have pulled out his own fingernails.

'She has been pretty sick. But you know Vivian, she'll fight to the last.'

The rush of love for her foster mother momentarily overcame the inexplicable...*oddness* she felt around this man.

The way he made her body feel suddenly unfamiliar to her—as though it were not quite her own.

Desperately trying to shake off the crazy notion, she forced another bright smile.

'And she's had Ruby and me, so she hasn't had to do it alone. But don't let her catch you talking about her behind her back. Grown adult or not, she'll give you *what for* and ground you for a week.'

'I don't doubt it.' Connor laughed, a deep sound that seemed to fill up the tiny kitchen, and seemed to somehow set Nell's skin alive with a delicious energy. 'Fortunately, right now Vivian's instructing Ivan and Ruby on some stall she wants them to build for the upcoming village fete.'

'Yup.' Nell nodded with a grin of her own. 'She wants them to do a photobooth, with pictures of the locals as well as Little Meadwood. I think I'm supposed to be doing a vintage clothing booth or something. I'm surprised she hasn't found something for you, too.'

'Oh, she's trying,' he confirmed.

'Ah well, since you live and work so far away with the army, you get to dodge that bullet.' Nell, laughing, was pretending she didn't feel the slightest bit disappointed at the idea that when he walked out of the door later, that would likely be the last time she'd see him.

He hadn't returned to Little Meadwood in decades, so he was hardly going to start visiting regularly now.

'Actually, I left the army.'

'Oh?' That shocked her. 'Does Vivian know?'

He gave a wry chuckle, causing a warmth to emanate from the tips of her fingers to the very soles of her feet. Like every time he smiled at her, or crinkled his eyes with laughter, it made her wonder if there was someone out there who got to see and experience that every day.

Which was even more ridiculous.

'No, I haven't mentioned it to Vivian yet.' His voice dragged her back to the present. 'I only left a few months ago.'

'Why?' The question was out before she'd even thought about it. 'Vivian always said the army was your life.'

The expression on his face turned instantly shuttered. Stark, even. His leaving didn't appear to have been his choice. Or, at least, not entirely.

'Life moves on,' he clipped out, clearly shutting her down. 'I work as a locum surgeon in a civilian hospital now.'

'Nearby?'

His jaw pulled tighter. She could see it.

'Other side of the country,' he gritted out.

Clearly that was deliberate. A host of additional

questions swirled around her head but Nell bit her tongue. It was apparent this wasn't a subject that Connor wanted to discuss.

Nell searched for something else to say instead.

'I still can't believe you and Ivan were so close. He was quite closed off when I first arrived here. I thought it was just the way he was. Now I suspect it was because he was missing his mate.'

For a moment, she thought Connor wasn't going to answer. Then, slowly, he dipped his head in confirmation.

'Maybe, we came from similar circumstances that we bonded, I guess. I might have been the same way if the situation had been reversed.' His voice was tight, as though he wasn't accustomed to talking about his past. 'Anyway, I gather that all three of you spent time here together?'

'Yeah, Ivan and I were long-term foster kids.' Remembering the tea, Nell busied herself around the kitchen as she spoke. 'When I arrived he was fifteen and I was thirteen. My parents had just died in a car accident.'

'Sorry for your loss,' Connor acknowledged simply. Sincerely.

Sadness clenched at her stomach as it always did when someone mentioned her parents. No longer raw, as it had been for years after their deaths, but there all the same, especially since she hadn't been ready for the memory.

Everyone in Little Meadwood knew her history,

they never really mentioned her parents any more—it was one of the comforts of staying in this small community. Although Jonathon had never understood that—he'd always accused her of using the village to *hide* away from facing the real world.

Nell thrust the unwanted thought from her head, and concentrated on pouring milk into the tea mugs.

'Thanks,' she managed instead, using banal facts to push through her tight cheerfulness. 'Anyway, Ruby arrived for the first time a few months later and she and I grew close instantly. Ivan left a year or so later, but Ruby was backwards and forwards for years. Her mum was ill, so whenever she needed to go into hospital for treatment, or an operation, Ruby would be fostered here. Sometimes it was just for a few nights, other times it could be weeks or a couple of months.'

'I see. I just thought that he and Ruby seem to know each other more recently, that was all.'

Nell jerked her head up. So he'd noticed that, too? She shouldn't be surprised: Connor Mason gave the impression that he spotted everything and missed nothing. Perhaps she ought to ask Ruby about it tonight when they were on their own and back in the cottage next door that they had shared ever since they'd officially left Vivian's care.

But for now, Nell lapsed into a thoughtful silence amidst the electric atmosphere that could only be Connor's presence. She tried to rally herself as she finished stirring the tea before setting the mugs on a tray to take through.

'To answer your earlier question about how Vivian really is, when she isn't pretending nothing is wrong at all, let me just say that Vivian is just being *Vivian*.'

'Understood.' His grin returned unexpectedly, and Nell wished her chest didn't thud so hard at the pleasure of it. 'In other words, if her arm was cut off, she'd claim it was just a scratch.'

'She would.' Nell laughed.

And this time it was a brilliant smile that was so genuine and unrestrained, and filled with such affection that it made Nell's chest pull tight. Tight enough that, just for a moment, tiny stars flashed in her head.

She scrambled to pull herself together.

'Anyway, it sounded as though you and Vivian were having a good chat.'

'We were,' he agreed, reaching to the tray to take a drink for her, and one for himself. 'It was...nice.'

'Right. Good.' They lapsed into another silence, with only the sound of the clinking porcelain to break the tension. And she took the opportunity to try to get a handle on her crazy reactions to him. 'Are you intending to stay long?'

'Here, you mean? Tonight?'

'In Little Meadwood in general,' she clarified.

His expression closed down abruptly, and he

didn't answer straight away. Instead, he seemed to take a moment to organise his thoughts.

'I hadn't planned to.'

'Initially the plan had been to call in and see her tonight and then…that was it?' she supplied evenly, but he still cast her a sharp gaze.

'My life is hectic,' he bit out sharply. 'I'm usually travelling.'

'I wasn't judging.' She held up her hands quickly.

Had she been? She hoped not. She'd learned long ago not to judge people. You never knew what another person might be dealing with.

'Right.' He blew out a breath and at least he had the grace to look a little rueful. 'The point is, that was the plan. But now…'

Nell waited for him to continue, telling herself it was of no matter to her what he chose to do; that her heart hadn't picked up a beat. Again.

He didn't answer, but instead raked a hand through his hair whilst the muscles in his jaw clenched. It was a trait that was already becoming familiar to her.

'But now that you've seen her, you don't want to leave?' she suggested at last.

'Pretty much,' he agreed tightly.

'She has that effect.' Nell smiled fondly.

'But I can't stay. I have a job across the country, and I have to be there for it. I just…don't like the idea of her being here alone and going through everything.'

'She isn't alone, though. I'm here,' Nell pointed out gently, 'as is Ruby. And now Ivan has arrived.'

Connor dipped his head in assent, but didn't look wholly convinced.

'I understand, but… I thought I might rent a house, or something. Pay for a full-time carer to be on hand. And it could be somewhere I can stay when I come back to visit.'

And she told herself there was no reason for this revelation to send a flurry of sensations skittering inside her.

'There's nothing in the village to rent,' Nell pointed out, hoping her tone was even. Level.

Connor frowned.

'Nothing? There were always cottages to rent here. In fact, you couldn't give them away.'

'Things have changed over the last twenty years.' Nell shrugged lightly. 'Both Upper and Little Meadwood are now part of the commuter belt and loads of people live here but work in the city. They even built a housing estate of about two thousand houses just outside over to the east.'

'I know, I saw it earlier,' he acknowledged grimly. 'Looks a monstrosity.'

'Then you should see what they charge for them.' She snorted. 'And they still elicit bidding wars every time one goes onto the market.'

'I can't have Vivian here alone. And whilst you all might be here in the area, you aren't *here*.'

'Not in this cottage, no,' Nell agreed. 'But Ruby

and I do live in the village. In fact, we live in the cottage next door.'

'Next door?'

And there was no reason for his voice to rumble through her the way that it did.

Instead, she forced a proud nod.

'I bought it ten years ago, luckily enough—for a reasonable price, since the new A road hadn't been built then.'

'You stayed in Little Meadwood?' Connor's frown deepened. 'After coming to Vivian?'

'I left when I was eighteen to do my training, but as soon as I could get a job at City Hospital, I came back.'

'Why?'

She paused, not quite understanding his question.

'I don't follow.'

He raked his hand through his hair again.

'Why on earth would you want to stay somewhere as small, as parochial, as Little Meadwood?'

'Maybe because I don't find it parochial,' she pointed out gently, refusing to take offence.

'It's small, and insular, and petty,' he ground out, before clamping his jaw closed as though he hadn't intended her to hear any of that.

She filed it away.

'Despite the circumstances of being a foster kid, I loved it here,' she offered carefully. 'Though I get that some foster kids couldn't wait to get away.'

'Not from Vivian,' he growled. 'Just this place.'

'Again, not judging.'

'So why did you stay?'

'I guess I found it friendly. Safe. *Home.*' The word thick in her throat. It meant more than she could express. 'Ruby felt the same. As did another foster girl around at the same time as us, Steph.'

Nell stopped abruptly, wondering what had made her mention this to a perfect stranger like Connor.

Perhaps because he didn't feel like a perfect stranger—the false lull of having both been Vivian's foster kids, no doubt.

Or maybe something else?

'Want to talk?'

The question was a gentle invitation but not pushy. And even though she suspected she should deflect, she found herself meeting his gaze.

'Steph was our friend,' Nell began slowly. 'Mine and Ruby's. She arrived after Ivan had left so we were here at the same time, though, as I said, Ruby was in and out of here, and home, depending on when her mum needed support during her chemo.'

His expression changed instantly to empathy.

'This must be particularly hard for Ruby, watching Vivian, then.'

'I think so,' Nell agreed. 'But she hides it well. She always says we all have unenviable pasts or we wouldn't have ended up foster kids.'

Connor inclined his head a fraction.

'Anyway, the three of us became inseparable. The Three Macesketeers.'

'Ah, *Mace*sketeers, as in Vivian *Macey.*' He understood at once.

Something rippled through her, but she chose not to examine it too closely. As it was, she didn't care to properly examine why she was still spilling personal details to this newcomer.

'So even after we'd transitioned out of the system, we all wanted to stay close. When I bought the cottage and moved back, they moved in with me.'

'Until Steph suddenly left.' He dipped his head, putting it together quickly.

A sharp pain stabbed at her.

'Three years ago. Abruptly, and with no explanation.'

Yet even though she didn't add how much that hurt, Connor somehow seemed to pick up on it.

'Sometimes people just need to move on. It doesn't mean there was something you did or didn't do.'

She blinked at him, startled.

'I know, but I can't help feeling there was something I could have done. Said.'

'Maybe.' He inclined his head. 'But maybe not. You've reached out to her, I take it?'

'Several times,' Nell confirmed sadly. 'Both of us. But we only ever get superficial replies. That she's fine. That one day we'll meet and catch up.'

'But even though she has been to visit Vivian, you haven't seen her?'

'Not once.'

And it hurt, even though she and Ruby both pretended it was fine.

'So a part of you is hoping that maybe Vivian's illness might finally bring you all back together.'

Nell blinked, staring at him.

How could he possibly know that? She hadn't even confided it to Ruby, as though doing so would somehow make it seem as though a horrible part of her welcomed Vivian's illness.

'You don't need to feel guilty.' Connor narrowed his eyes thoughtfully at her. 'You're not wishing anything on Vivian. Her illness is there—it has already happened. You're just looking for those tiny silver linings in life that we all hope for. It's part of what makes us human.'

'Well…' she shrugged, as if she could also shrug off any residual lapse in judgement '…anyway, the point is that I like living here. It's a bit of a commute to the hospital, but not too bad. Certainly worth it.'

Without warning, the silence dropped again; though she wasn't sure what she had said to cause it.

She took a sip of tea in the hope of steadying the nerves that had once again started jangling. Then, after what felt like an age, Connor spoke.

'That's what Vivian just said.'

'Ah.' Nell took another careful sip of tea and pretended her stomach didn't flip-flop.

So, Vivian had already tried to put ideas in Connor's head. The question was, would he be interested enough to listen?

A part of her couldn't help hoping so, although Nell couldn't explain what it was—this pull that seemed to keep drawing her to the man.

She was determined not to ask any more. It wasn't any of her business.

'Are you thinking about staying, then?' The words slid out despite her efforts.

His gaze was trained out of the window for the longest time.

'She was ostensibly talking about Ivan—apparently he transferred to a temporary post at City Hospital last week?' He paused as if for confirmation, so Nell nodded.

She still didn't know exactly why Ivan had stayed, but she sensed it was what he and Ruby were so intent about. Not that she was about to confide that part to Connor on top of everything else.

'Vivian suggested I might consider a temporary post in their emergency trauma department, too.'

His eyes slid to hers all too tellingly, his expression so neutral that it was almost comical, and Nell felt a gurgle of laughter rumble up inside her.

'Vivian merely suggested it?' Her lips tugged up at the corners. 'She hasn't already called them to demand they create a vacancy?'

'She suggested it,' he repeated dryly. 'Strongly. Like I said, I haven't yet had a chance to tell her that I've left the army.'

This time, they both chuckled. Vivian Macey had always been an infamous tour de force.

'Good luck with that.' Nell chuckled. 'She'll have you here even if it means you sleeping on that tiny couch in the living room.'

'I've endured worse.' He grinned and lifted one muscular shoulder. 'I've been locuming and couch or hotel surfing as it is.'

Her heart thumped loudly against her ribcage. Once. Twice. Her mouth felt inexplicably dry.

'So you're actually considering it?'

She didn't care either way.

Definitely not.

Her heart offered another thump of betrayal as Connor's eyes held hers, intense and unwavering, and Nell found herself holding her breath. She couldn't shake the impression that the room was suddenly closing in on her—on both of them—and yet it was far from an unpleasant sensation.

'The contract at the hospital I'm currently at is due to expire and I was planning on moving on anyway,' he said finally, breaking the silence.

'They don't want you to renew?' she managed to ask.

'Yes, but I have no intention of taking up their offer.'

'So you could move up this way?' She had no idea how she managed to keep her voice level. 'If you wanted to.'

There was a sudden shift in the air between them, a charged tension that Nell couldn't quite explain but couldn't ignore either.

'I'm…considering it.'

What was it that made a man like Connor tick? In the short time she'd known him, she'd already felt ridiculously drawn to him—and she could tell herself that it was just their shared experience of being foster kids, and having Vivian as a foster parent, but deep down she felt it was more than that.

Ivan had the same experience, and she'd never felt drawn to him the way she did with this particular man.

Watching Connor over the rim of her mug, his expression as unreadable as ever, she couldn't help but wonder what was going through his mind. What had led him to leave Little Meadwood for the army when he hadn't even been sixteen, and what had spurred him to leave the forces now after Vivian had recently read that he'd just been honoured with some prestigious military commendation?

Connor Mason was a closely guarded mystery. And she had more than enough to occupy her time without taking on yet another puzzle to solve.

No matter how tempting this particular conundrum might be.

Forcing herself to look away, she set her mug down on the table between them. She should probably take the drinks through to the others before they got cold.

'Well.' She plastered a cheerful smile on her lips. 'I'm sure you're capable of making your own decisions.'

The expression on Connor's face was as indecipherable as ever.

'Indeed,' he told her, his voice neutral as he got smoothly to his feet. 'Thank you for the tea. It's time I got going.'

So soon?

'What about Vivian?' she asked quickly.

'I have a feeling she was beginning to get a little tired in there with all of us, which is another reason why I came in here—to give her some space. I feel she would benefit from some rest.'

It shouldn't have been such a battle to stuff down the sense of disappointment, and simply nod her agreement.

'But come back tomorrow.' The words spilled out before she could stop them. 'It was clear Vivian loved seeing you.'

'I'm back on duty tomorrow.' He shook his head.

'After duty, then?'

'One hundred and fifty miles away.'

'Of course.' And there was no reason for her insides to tumble like that—as though a part of her was disappointed. No reason at all. 'You did mention it was across the country.'

'Anyway, I should have twenty-four hours' downtime after my next shift, so I'll make another quick visit then. And another a couple of days after that.'

Nell's stomach flip-flopped. She pretended not to notice.

'That's quite a drive.'

He dipped his head, looking unconcerned.

'It's a couple of hours each way on the motorbike. The ride clears my head.'

Even so, after long shifts at the hospital he would soon be exhausted.

'Can't you stay in a hotel at least?' she asked. 'Ride back tomorrow?'

He shook his head tersely, though all he said was, 'Hate hotels.'

The clipped tightness warned her not to ask questions. Even so, his tone revealed more than she suspected he had intended. What must it be like to be one of the few that a man like Connor would trust enough to confide in?

She thrust the thought aside. She would never be one of those few—and she had no idea why she would even want to be.

Liar, a voice whispered in her head. So, she thrust that away, too.

She could always offer Connor use of the sofa at her and Ruby's cottage next door—Ivan had slept there a couple of times the previous month, before he'd found his own lodgings in the city—but her throat suddenly turned dry and the words didn't come. As ridiculous as it might be, it somehow felt different offering this man a bed for the night than it had felt offering the same thing to Ivan. And she could tell herself that it was because she'd actually known Ivan when they'd both been Vivian's foster kids whilst, technically, she'd only just met Connor, but the truth was it was more than that. A different feeling in her gut. A draw that she didn't care to try to explain.

Nell was grateful when Connor abruptly broke the silence.

'Anyway, I really should get going.'

'Right,' she managed awkwardly. 'Well, safe ride. Take it easy.'

Take it easy?

But Connor was already crossing the small space, his hand on the door handle. For a brief moment he paused, as if he was going to say something else before he changed his mind. The next moment, he was gone—back into the living room.

And by the time Nell had loaded the mugs and Vivian's cup on a tray, adding a few of Vivian's favourite mini-cakes—even though her foster mother's illness meant that she couldn't really enjoy them any more—Connor was already out of the door and revving up his beloved motorbike.

Leaving Little Meadwood as quickly as he'd apparently entered it. And for the sake of her galloping heart, that was surely a good thing.

Wasn't it?

CHAPTER FOUR

TEN FORTY-EIGHT AND it had been a particularly hectic shift in Resus so far. No sooner had Nell and her team managed to clear one patient out of the bays, than another two arrived.

But at least she loved her work—and at least being slammed meant she didn't have time to dwell on things that she really shouldn't be dwelling on.

As if things were completely normal.

As if she hadn't spent the past two weeks fighting the odd notion that life at Little Meadwood had somehow been nudged out of kilter ever since Connor Mason's unexpected arrival.

As if she weren't still fighting her mind from wandering back to that distracting evening with him. The one and only time she had met the man who she had grown up thinking of as some kind of an unspoken legend around Vivian's home.

Was it really only a mere fortnight ago? It felt like a lifetime.

And if being in that kitchen with him had felt like sticking her hand into an electric socket, then the subsequent absence of contact had only amplified that thing she chose to call *nervousness*, which coursed through her veins.

It certainly didn't help that she'd visited Vivian several evenings after work, only to discover that Connor had already been there earlier in the day but left before she'd arrived. She'd spotted him once, from a distance. He'd looked a little more exhausted than that first time, though no less sexy for it. No less arresting.

It really shouldn't be allowed that his slightly tousled look only made him all the more attractive. Perhaps that was why it was proving impossible to get him out of her head. Memories lingered of that tall, broad, mouth-wateringly muscular physique, and that voice, which was as smooth and deep as molten chocolate—no matter how hard she tried to eject them.

Just as she was trying and failing to do right now. And she couldn't help wondering if Connor had been avoiding her.

Which has to make you the most ridiculously self-absorbed person in Little Meadwood, a scornful voice instantly piped up in her head. *Possibly the country.*

Shame flushed through Nell's body. Hot. Restless. It made her clench her hands in her lap and struggle to even out her shallow, rapid breaths.

She needed to get a grip; Connor was only here to visit their foster mother. To think anything different was pure self-centredness. And still, no matter how quickly she found herself racing home after work and into Vivian's, the man had always *just left*. Her heart picked up its pace inside her chest.

It was almost a relief when the shrill ring of the Resus emergency phone rent the air, and even as Nell snatched it up she could feel the department swinging to life behind her.

'City Hospital,' she clipped out efficiently, instantly tuning into the case that was being relayed to her.

A few pertinent questions later, confident she had all the information available at that moment, she quickly set about putting a call over the Tannoy system to call her team.

Ten fifty-nine. Nell noted the clock on the wall. *The heli would be here within the next sixteen minutes.*

'Okay, guys, listen in. Patient is a female in her forties; sudden-onset thunderclap headache and a GCS of three, now hypertensive. ETA is fifteen minutes. Allie, can you get a CT scanner put on standby? Kris, can you advise Neurology?'

The acknowledgements were instantaneous as the team bustled around preparing the bay for their patient.

Nell's heart kicked in her chest, keeping the adrenalin coursing around her body. This was the tensest part—the waiting. Only having the basic details for the patient, and waiting to see exactly what state they were going to be in. Waiting to do her job.

But at least this kept her mind busy…and away from certain grey-eyed individuals.

Her eyes flitted to the well-equipped tray that ensured the most likely tools would be to hand, the glistening mattress still fresh from the Steri-wipe but that would be dry in minutes, and the monitors with their lines just waiting to be hooked up to their patient.

Everything was ready.

'What have we got?'

The voice appeared around the curtain, fractions of a second before the material moved. But in those millionths of a second, a myriad emotions shot through Nell faster than any rush of adrenalin. Her heart kicked again—but this time for a very different reason. She turned carefully, fighting the urge to whip around. This had to be her imagination playing some nonsensical prank.

It wasn't.

Connor?

'Nell.'

She wasn't sure if she was gratified or not that he looked as surprised as she was.

'You're working here now?'

She didn't know why she should feel so surprised—*shocked*, even. He might have been adamant about not leaving his locum post part-way across the country, but she could well imagine the toll taken by those past couple of weeks of making that torturously long round trip. And at least he looked as caught off guard as she felt.

'I thought it better to be on hand for Vivian,' he rasped.

But then his expression shifted and smoothed, though not before she thought she glimpsed a flash of guilt.

Of course, he'd at least known that she worked at this hospital. And Ruby, and Ivan, she reminded herself hastily. He could have mentioned it to any one of them—not necessarily just her.

'A heads-up would have been nice,' she heard herself clip out, all the same.

'I didn't expect it to happen so fast,' he replied in what might have been an approximation of an apology. Or maybe not. 'My former boss was more understanding than I would have thought.'

She wanted to ask what else he had expected. It had only taken a few Internet searches—which she was telling herself were out of professional interest and nothing more—to reveal that Connor Mason was a decorated veteran whose innovation in the field had led to the army modifying at least two of its approaches to treating wounded soldiers. Any hospital chief would want a man like Connor Mason on their rotas, and if his foster mother was ill and needed him to move close by only a short-sighted boss would stand in his way.

Or perhaps that was just because Connor had spent so many years following orders. No doubt the chief of the hospital Connor had just left was banking on a show of compassion and support to lure Connor back after Vivian…well, after his presence in Little Meadwood was no longer necessary.

Nell's heart kicked for a third time as she thrust that unwanted thought from her head. She scrambled for something more banal to say instead.

'Well, you're here now so you might as well know that patient is a female in her forties with sudden onset thunderclap headache…'

And she gave a silent word of thanks for the distraction as she reeled off the remaining scant details to him, as well as letting him know she'd advised Neurology and CT.

'Understood.' He inclined his head in tacit approval.

But anything else she might have said was sucked from her head as the Resus doors opened and the Heli-med crew clattered in with their patient, and her team sprung to action taking the handover, changing beds, and setting up the monitoring equipment. It was several minutes before the verbal handover could take place. But at length, the Heli-doctor began.

'This is Annabel, forty-three, an estate agent. Around forty minutes ago she was working at her desk when she suffered a sudden onset thunderclap headache, quickly became unintelligible before sliding to the floor and becoming unresponsive. When we arrived she had a Glasgow Coma Scale of three, this increased to seven and she vomited several times in the air ambulance.'

The handover continued as the team carried out their own checks, hooking their patient up to their own monitors and trying to establish the situation.

'And her blood pressure now?' Nell verified, when it was complete, craning to see the readouts over the sea of heads.

One of the nurses closer to the monitor pushed the screen a little higher and a rush of adrenalin coursed through Nell.

'Right, let's get her to the scanner,' Connor cut in abruptly, causing Nell to turn to him.

'She seems quite restless and agitated.' She pursed her lips. 'Do you think we can risk it?'

'I think time isn't on our side,' he answered.

He had a point. If it was a ruptured brain aneurysm, then the sooner it was diagnosed, the better. The first few hours would be vital.

'Okay, let's get her to CT,' Nell concurred. 'Everybody ready to move her?'

Connor moved in beside her. 'Good. On three; one, two, go.'

The next half-hour was a race against time as Nell and her team hurried their patient to CT and got as clear images as they could. Despite their patient not being entirely still, the images were enough to confirm her and Connor's suspicion that she had a significant subarachnoid haemorrhage.

At least now they could begin to administer medication that would help lower the woman's blood pressure, ready for her transfer to the neurosurgical team who would carry out the aneurysm clipping.

Exhausted but relieved, Nell stripped her gown and gloves off, turning around to check the surprisingly quiet Resus ward…and slammed straight into Connor.

'Oof. Sorry.' Nell quashed the kick of traitorous flip-flopping in her chest.

'Not a problem. Good work there, by the way.'

And she told herself that she hated that *oh-so-casually-sexy* way about him he had that made her whole body sizzle. Yet she didn't make any attempt to carry on walking.

Then again, neither did he.

'I should have told you I was starting work here,' he acknowledged after a pause that might just as easily been a moment or a lifetime. 'Like I said, it really did all happen so quickly.'

'So today is your first day?'

'It is.'

'Oh.' She hadn't really expected him to agree.

At least it meant that he hadn't been here for a week or something without even thinking to mention it to any of the rest of them. And although the initial kicks had subsided, her heart was still beating out its humiliating tattoo.

It seemed too cruel that her stomach chose that moment to rumble again, then growl. Loudly.

This time there was no stopping her body's reactions as she felt the heat bloom across her cheeks. She quickly pressed her hand down harder in the vain hope that she could silence its embarrassing protestations.

'My shift started at seven and I missed my break because it's been mayhem down here,' she garbled even as she told herself that she didn't owe him any explanation.

Connor, however, simply offered a casual dip of a shoulder.

'Occupational hazard. You haven't eaten at all?'

'No, so I should probably grab a sandwich now that it's a little quieter again.'

He consulted his watch.

'You must be starving. I'll walk with you if you've got a moment.'

'Oh. No. I…'

But either he didn't hear her, or he chose to ignore her hesitation.

'Where's a good place to grab a bite? I seem to recall seeing various cafés in the atrium back there.'

And even though she opened her mouth to object—because getting lunch with Connor suddenly felt like a ridiculously dangerous idea—she heard herself telling him that they were all decent eateries.

'Although Re-Cup-Eration is my favourite.' Her mouth was still moving, despite her efforts to stop it. 'It's a great place, and they have a nice selection of good food. I…was just heading over there.'

'Great, lead on.'

Firmly telling herself that it meant nothing, Nell led the way out of Resus and down the corridor. Yet she was still acutely aware of Connor's presence beside her like a magnetic pull, tugging at her with every step they took. It was all she could do to stop herself from drifting closer, especially when she happened to glance over to him to find him looking at her with an intensity that made her already flushed cheeks feel even hotter.

Her brain scrabbled for a safer topic.

'Vivian must be really pleased you've taken up the post.'

'She doesn't know yet,' he confessed.

'So you aren't staying with her?'

Could he hear the thudding in her chest? Surely it was loud enough to drown out the entire hospital.

'No, I'm in hospital accommodation.'

'Really?' Nell pulled a face. 'It's okay, but wouldn't have thought you'd find it good enough.'

'I've lived in shelled-out ruins when in theatres of war.' He didn't appear to take offence. 'I can stay anywhere.'

A heat bloomed through her cheeks.

'Sorry, I forgot.'

'It isn't important.' He shrugged it off. 'But, as it is, the accommodation for senior staff is in some new apartment block across the fields at the back of the hospital.'

'Oh.' She just about restrained herself from

smacking her forehead with her hand. 'I'd forgotten about that place. It's new. And swanky.'

Should she have said that?

To her surprise, Connor nodded his head.

'Like a five-star luxury hotel.' He laughed. 'Apparently, I have a third-floor suite.'

A deep, genuine sound that seemed to spark all her senses. The kind of laugh that she realised she wanted to hear again, and again, and again. It made her wonder what it must be like to make this man smile, and laugh, *and love*, on a daily basis.

Crazy.

Nell shoved the errant thought from her mind and fought to steady her nerves. A thought occurred to her.

'Wait, didn't they evacuate the third floor yesterday?'

'Sorry?'

'Yes, I'm sure they did.' Her brain spun trying to recall what she'd overheard that morning from a surgeon she recognised but didn't know well. 'Apparently there's a fault with the sensor system on the third floor and it keeps going off every hour or so. No one on the third floor got any sleep last night. They've had to clear the suites whilst they find the faulty sensor so everyone has either swapped to work tonight's night shift or booked a hotel. You ought to call now or they'll be booked out.'

It was too late for him to swap his current shift to tonight. But then Connor's jaw tightened.

'Do you want me to recommend which places to try first?'

'No.' He shook his head. 'I'll just see if I can find an on-call room.'

'I don't think that will work—' she began but he cut her off.

'It will be fine.'

Except that he sounded anything but fine.

'Are you okay?'

'Never better,' he ground out.

Now she thought about it, hadn't she thought he'd reacted a little oddly last time hotels had been mentioned? But then she'd put it down to her imagination.

Nell bit her bottom lip uncertainly.

'You could always crash on our sofa.' Her heart wasn't clattering against her ribcage. It wasn't. 'Ruby won't mind, since she's away at the moment.'

'I'll be fine,' he declined quickly, before adding a terse, 'thank you, though.'

Evidently that was him shutting the conversation down. Only she couldn't let it go that easily.

'It isn't an issue; Ivan crashed with us for a few nights a couple of months ago.'

'Nonetheless.'

A wiser person might have let it go. And she would…after one more comment.

'Okay, but if you change your mind, I have a spare key. So does Vivian.'

'I won't but, again, thanks.'

This time there was no doubt that the subject was definitely closed, and they descended into silence for the rest of the short walk to Re-Cup-Eration. But once they entered the soaring glass-and-metal atrium, Nell felt lifted again—just as the bright, plant-filled space had been designed to do. Leading the way across the polished stone floor, she skirted the smaller carts and stations, as well as the more than acceptable Tyler's Café, and to Re-Cup-Eration.

'I don't think I've sat down to eat in months,' Connor commented casually, picking up a laminated menu from one of the free tables and skimming it. 'The hospital I've come from only has one cafeteria, and it's always hectic.'

'No restaurants for dates in the evenings?'

Nell's stomach dropped even as the words left her lips. All the blood seemed to rush from her body and pool in her feet—what the heck was she doing asking him about *dates*?

But incredibly, Connor didn't seem to notice.

'No time recently.' He lifted one shoulder a fraction. 'It's been sandwich vans, salad bars and microwave meals all the way.'

'Right,' she managed.

'So, what's good?' He lifted his eyes from the menu to lock with hers.

Nell struggled to ignore the answering *zing* inside her. He was just making conversation; it didn't make this any kind of *date*.

What was wrong with her?

With a superhuman effort, she pulled herself together.

'Everything here is good,' she told him sincerely. 'But right now, they do an amazing ploughman's hot panini with mature cheddar, sun-ripened tomatoes, and a homemade chutney. And their Sweet, Sour 'n' Crispy Salad has pomegranate seeds and the most incredible balsamic vinegars. It's the perfect blend of sweet and sour and is to die for. That's what I'm getting anyway.'

Was she waffling? She felt as if she was waffling.

'Okay, two lots of ploughman's panini and Sweet, Sour, 'n' Crispy Salad it is, then,' he confirmed, selecting a tray and placing it down on the serving rail as Nell tried to stop herself from ridiculously reading too much into the fact that he'd followed her recommendations to the letter. 'What drink? And do you want to get a table for us?'

'You can't buy my lunch.' Nell just about managed not to squeak at the prospect of sitting down and eating lunch with the man.

As if she'd never eaten with any other man in her life.

As if it were some kind of date.

'Call it a thank you for being there for Vivian all these years,' he answered simply.

'But…'

'Nothing more than that,' he added, silencing her objection.

Of course not. Nell struggled to regulate her wayward thoughts.

'Right,' she managed. 'Well, then, thank you, I'll just have a bottle of water, please.'

And then, before she could let her thoughts scatter off again, she turned and headed for one of the quieter, out-of-the-way tables.

Not because she wanted to be alone with Connor, she told herself hastily, but because she didn't want all her colleagues seeing them together, and then making them a hot topic on the hospital grapevine.

Whatever it was about this man that had her acting so uncharacteristically, it needed to stop.

By the time Connor appeared with their lunch, Nell was confident she'd sorted her thoughts, and her head was back in order.

She thanked him again as he placed the tray down with their meals and slid into the seat opposite her, then busied herself with the plates.

A few moments later, she took a bite of her panini, and let the tangy deliciousness of the chutney and sharpness of the melted cheese transport her momentarily out of the hospital and to somewhere far more relaxing.

'So how long have you worked here?' Connor asked, drawing her back to the present.

'Almost eight years. I went to uni when I left Vivian's care at eighteen, though she always kept her littlest spare room for me to crash with her every other weekend, and in the holidays.' Nell smiled warmly.

'Really? I never realised she stopped fostering.'

'Vivian didn't stop fostering,' she admitted. 'Did you know she received an MBE for fostering one hundred and fifty kids?'

'I had no idea.'

It was his clear guilt at the idea that he hadn't kept in touch enough that caused something to shift inside Nell.

'Anyway, she kept my room for me, and in return I helped out with other foster kids every other weekend.'

'So you returned to help with the other foster kids.' He nodded in understanding. 'That was generous of you.'

'My ex-fiancé didn't think so.'

Nell clamped her mouth shut, shocked at her admission. Or at least, shocked that she'd voiced it to Connor, of all people.

'You were engaged?'

She wished she could understand that unreadable expression on his face.

'For a year,' she heard herself tell him. 'He was a surgeon at the hospital where I was training.'

'And he didn't like you helping Vivian with the fostering?'

She pulled a face.

'Not so much that…' She tailed off. 'It's complicated.'

Which was an excuse, and she knew Connor knew that. But she certainly wasn't going to tell him that the truth was that Jonathon had always felt she'd been doing it for the wrong reasons. He'd felt Little Meadwood was her safety net—a world she'd retreated into after her parents' deaths—and that fostering was her excuse to race back there and out of the 'real world', as he'd called it.

'Is that why he's your ex-fiancé?' Connor asked instead, after the silence had stretched that little bit longer between them.

Nell lifted her shoulders in feigned casualness.

'He was offered a promotion in a hospital across the country. It was too good an opportunity to pass up.'

No need to add that he'd found her a great opportunity too, she just hadn't wanted to be that far from Little Meadwood. That made it seem as though Jonathon had been right about the village being her 'crutch'.

And clearly that wasn't true.

'Sorry that happened to you,' Connor offered, evidently assuming her ex-fiancé had just upped and left her.

Nell cranked out a bright smile.

'Don't be. I had just been offered a job here, and I'd managed to buy the cottage next door to Vivian. So everything worked out well.'

'This place is lucky to have you. You're very good at what you do,' Connor told her in that low, gravelly voice that seemed to scrape deliciously somewhere deep inside her.

'Thank you.' She managed a rueful smile. 'Though I don't feel good right now. I have a case that's bugging me for some reason, but I can't understand why.'

'Oh?' She wasn't surprised that he looked instantly intrigued. 'What's the case?'

She wrinkled her nose, trying to order her thoughts. She had nothing more than a gut feeling that something was *off* about the case, but none of the tests had supported her doubts and the rest of her team had let it go. Yet still, she couldn't seem to.

'In a way it isn't so much that it's just one case, but two. They aren't identical but I can't shake the feeling that they're just a bit too similar.'

'Go on,' he encouraged when she trailed off.

She drew in a deep breath.

'Two girls presented on different weekends. One last weekend, one this weekend. Both had been at a nightclub drinking when they fell unconscious. Each girl's friends report that neither had had much to drink but out of nowhere one of them stopped making sense when she talked, and the other simply lost the ability to stand. Both girls only had drinks from bottles and covered the tops, and there's no CCTV suggesting their drinks got spiked.'

'No memory?'

'One girl describes it like a black hole in her brain. But out of nowhere, you know? One minute she seemed fine and normal, dancing with her friends; the next moment everything is gone.'

'And toxicology?' Connor asked thoughtfully.

'Nothing indicative, but then given that some drugs are designed to leave the body in under twelve hours, it's possible that by the time we realised the circumstances and tested, we were already too late.'

'Unfortunately, that happens,' he acknowledged. 'Did you check for puncture marks? Needle marks.'

Nell stared at him for a moment.

'Needle marks?' She realised slowly. 'You think they might have been spiked by injection?'

'It's becoming a big problem in the hospital I've just left.'

'Now you mention it, I've heard of cases up and down the country.' She nodded. 'But we hadn't seen it here before. I didn't even think—it's just too awful.'

'It is,' he agreed grimly. 'So when you get the chance, see if your patient will let you check her over. Could be anywhere, and it will be tiny. But I've often found them on backs of legs, or backside. Fleshier areas that a patient wouldn't be able to see for themselves.'

'Right. Will do.' She fell into silence for a moment as she contemplated the ramifications of it.

How many more patients might begin to present themselves at City Hospital? What if those victims didn't have friends around looking out for them? She couldn't decide whether she wanted to find telltale needle marks or not.

Well, she would have to deal with that issue if and when it arose again. It wouldn't help anybody if she started to fall into that particular rabbit hole right now.

Pulling herself back to the present, Nell summoned a bright smile as she turned back to Connor.

'You should know that Vivian's never made any secret of how proud she is of the way you worked your way through the ranks to become a surgeon.'

As far as pivots went, that had hardly been graceful, but she refused to regret it. Even if Connor's expression turned distant for a moment.

'That isn't exactly how it works.'

'It's how Vivian tells it.' Nell lifted her hands in silent apology. 'I just know you signed up the very day of your sixteenth birthday.'

Connor cast another tight expression, then appeared to relent.

'True enough, I suppose. Strictly speaking, I started the application process the moment I could a few months earlier and, because I was so adamant, Vivian used her contacts and convinced a colonel and his wife to take me in for those last few months to help me get ready for it.'

'I never knew any of that.' Nell shook her head.

Interestingly, she felt her response seemed to ease some of the tension in his body language.

'Oh. Well.' He took a bite of his food and she couldn't help wondering if he was buying some time to reorder his thoughts whilst he finished chewing. 'I was lucky that the colonel took me under his wing. He was tough, and keen on the kind of discipline that I really needed back then, but he also encouraged me to keep my studies going alongside the training, and he helped me to see that I had more options. Pretty much everything Vivian had tried to tell me, but I think I needed the army's *tough love* approach.'

Nell nodded. Somehow, she could see that about him.

'Actually, it was the colonel's widow who managed to track down the civvie hospital where I was working, to pass on the message that Vivian wasn't well.'

'Oh.' Nell blinked in surprise. She'd never thought to wonder how Connor had heard about their foster mother's situation.

'Anyway,' Connor brushed the topic aside, 'I ended up getting army sponsorship to study medicine at uni, and they took me to places like Canada, Cyprus and Belize to enhance my training.'

'According to Vivian, you were also in warzones.'

'I did several tours,' Connor confirmed, but there was a neutrality to his tone that warned her not to pry too deeply.

'Did you enjoy visiting places around the world?' She tried to keep her own tone light. 'I haven't visited Canada or Belize, although I've been on a bit of a girls' holiday to Cyprus, with Ruby and Steph.'

For a moment, Connor only eyed her intently. As though he were searching right inside her, rooting her to the thin plastic bucket seat.

'Yeah, I loved my time with the army. Did you know that Belize has stunning butterfly farms? Or that their national butterfly is the blue morpho?'

And she didn't think it was his imagination that he looked furious with himself for asking such questions. Was that…? Did he…? Was that some kind of reference to her eyes? Her entire life people had remarked on their colour and vividness, but it had never made her heart pound the way it was pounding now.

'I…didn't know that,' she confessed after a moment.

Connor cleared his throat and took a sip of his drink, his eyes flickering away from hers for a moment. Nell took the opportunity to do the same, taking a bite of her salad to give her mouth something to do besides ask him inappropriate questions about his time in the army.

They fell into a silence, both lost in their own thoughts. Nell couldn't help but feel a sense of intrigue surrounding Connor, coupled with a growing attraction that she wasn't sure what to do with. Eventually, it was Nell who broke the quiet.

'So now you're out of the military, and able to visit Vivian,' she pivoted cheerfully, relieved when the slightly darker shadow in his eyes lifted.

'I am.'

'Can I ask how long you intend to stay here at City?' she asked, taking a forkful of food as she pretended her heart hadn't suddenly picked up a beat at the question.

Connor didn't so much as shrug, but instead lightly extended the fingers of one hand.

'As long as Vivian needs me to.'

'Well, don't be surprised if Vivian throws you some "welcome home party".'

Nell had intended it as a little bit of light humour; she hadn't intended the distinct shift in his expression.

'She'd be the only one to attend.'

His tension was so unexpected and odd that she stared at him for a moment.

'Why would you say that?'

Connor met her gaze, and she could tell he wasn't going to answer her question directly.

'It's…complicated,' he admitted gruffly. 'Little Meadwood and I were never a good fit.'

That part surprised her.

'Even though your photo is up in the Willow Tree pub? And you're part of the annual winter toast.'

'Say again?' he demanded sharply, his eyes blazing. 'For what reason? As some kind of cautionary tale?'

'What?' Nell was confused by his sudden change in demeanour, her heart racing as she tried to think of what she might have said wrong. 'No, as one of the absent friends.'

'I seriously doubt that,' he growled.

'Why?' Nell asked instinctively. She paused, licking her lips. 'The photo is of you in your uniform. There's a photo of Ivan in his uniform, too. And one of Alison Tanner's son—I don't know if you remember him.'

'I do. Though I still don't...'

'Because you're all local heroes that the village is proud to call their own.' She shrugged.

'Then it certainly won't be me.' His voice was too even, too tightly controlled.

It hinted at churning waters beneath the apparently smooth exterior. Dark waters that hid so much.

And the thought of it tugged at her.

'It's you,' she confirmed in a low voice. 'Your pictures have been up for years. Everyone in the village knows about them. It seems it is only you who has a strangely low opinion of yourself.'

His eyes flashed at that.

'On the contrary,' he gritted out. 'Vivian taught me many things, but the most important of all was the ability to believe in myself.'

'Because if we don't believe in ourselves then how can we expect others to?' Nell grinned as she quoted their foster mother perfectly.

It was a lesson she suspected Vivian had tried to instil in all her charges. But though he didn't answer, Connor's gaze flickered away from hers and his expression was oddly perturbed. A yawning ache opened up inside Nell's chest.

And even though she warned herself not to be so ridiculous, she couldn't help wishing she understood this enigmatic man better. At least she was no longer resenting him for the idea that he was swooping in to take control after all these years—or lying to herself that it was the reason Connor Mason got under her skin.

But was that better, or worse? Nell couldn't tell. And as the conversation shifted to work, their experiences in the medical field, and even a few shared stories, Nell found herself feeling more and more comfortable in his presence.

There was no squashing the sense of disappointment that jolted through her when they realised that they'd been there for over half an hour. Definitely time to get back to work.

As they stood to leave, Connor's hand accidentally brushed against her—a small, innocent gesture, yet it sent another jolt of electricity through her body, causing her to pull her hand quickly away. The abruptness of her reaction seemed to catch them both by surprise.

'Sorry.'

Was it her imagination or did his voice sound different? There was a rasp that she was sure hadn't been there before, as though he was just as affected by the contact as she was. Just as caught off guard.

'It's fine.' She forced a smile, trying to play it off, but his eyes held hers a fraction too long and she knew they were both struggling to rebalance themselves.

The realisation was…*thrilling*.

Then, trays cleared to the side, they fell into step with each other as they made their way back to A & E, the only sound being the soft *schlep* of their trainers against the polished hospital floors.

'Thank you again for lunch.' Nell finally broke the silence.

She wasn't surprised when he waved it away.

'Nice not to eat on the hoof for once.'

Reaching A & E, he stepped forward to open the door for her and as she stepped through and thanked him those piercing silver-grey eyes of his caught hers and held her. Something indefinable in his expression sending delicious shivers down her spine and making her heart beat faster against her ribcage, especially when neither of them moved.

It was amazing how just that look from this man caused some song to start up deep inside her very core. She could feel that tension between them start to build again, and she couldn't help but wonder where it might lead. Even now, his eyes were scanning her face slowly, seeming to take in every feature before eventually flicking down to her lips. It was all she could do not to lick them.

The air between them felt so charged, so electric, that her entire body began to hum with anticipation. She had never been this attracted to anyone before, and it both terrified and exhilarated her. What might it be like to be held by this man? To be kissed? To be touched?

What might it be like if she leaned forward, just a few inches, and kissed him?

Before she could act on the impulse, Connor stepped back abruptly, breaking the spell and dispersing the tension.

'Take care, Nell,' he said softly, his voice rough with emotion, before turning and leaving the hospital.

Nell stood there for a moment, feeling as if something had been lost. Had she really been about to lean forward and kiss Connor Mason?

What had she even been thinking?

She shook herself out of her daze and headed back to work, her thoughts consumed with what might have *nearly* just happened between them.

And how she needed to make damned sure it didn't happen again.

CHAPTER FIVE

'HAVE YOU TAKEN the surgical role at City Hospital yet?' his foster mother demanded the instant he stepped through the familiar cottage door.

Connor didn't answer, instead focusing on helping his foster mum back down into her chair after she'd clearly exhausted herself with the effort of walking to open the front door.

'Well?' she pressed, once she was finally settled.

'And if I say I haven't?' he answered wryly. 'Or suggest that I don't have any intention of taking it?'

'Then I'd say you're being so stubborn,' Vivian huffed, if a little wheezily.

'Not stubborn,' he told her lightly, teasing her just as they had both done decades earlier. 'I just already have a job.'

'A job that's so far away that you're spending almost twelve hours a week travelling back and forth to see me.' Her eyes were full of concern. 'I know how you feel about staying in hotels, Connor, and I understand why. Perhaps it would be better if you didn't visit me so often.'

'Out of the question.' His humour evaporated in an instant. Though it was gratifying to see the flash of pleasure in her gaze, even if it didn't erase the concerned expression. 'For the record, I contacted City Hospital last week. I started there today.'

'You've moved back here?' Vivian actually attempted to shift herself into a more upright position, her shrewd gaze pinning him—just as it had once used to do. 'What precipitated that change of heart?'

'You did.' He grinned.

'And who else?' Vivian snorted and he revelled in the sound. It suddenly felt like...*home.*

Lunacy!

'No one else.' Connor cocked his eyebrows at her.

But oddly—though logic told him that was true—something shifted within him. As though Vivian wasn't entirely incorrect.

Swiftly, he shut down the image of Nell Parker that had popped inexplicably into his head.

'You still look tired, though.' Vivian's voice seeped back into his consciousness.

He turned to face his former foster mother, summoning another light-hearted grin.

'Thanks for that.'

A smile stole, unbidden, over his lips as another image popped back into his brain. He couldn't stop it; he'd enjoyed his lunch with Nell earlier. More than he'd expected to. And it kept replaying in his mind. Even now, he could picture her in surprising detail—like her eyes, which were as crystal-clear and sparklingly aquamarine as the waters around the Bahamas where he'd once snorkelled.

Would Nell enjoy snorkelling?

What was wrong with him?

It was as bad as his inadvertent butterfly comments. It should concern him more that he hadn't been able to help himself. As if she had woven some kind of bizarre spell over him ever since that first day when they'd met out on the road, and then right here in this very cottage only a matter of weeks ago. She'd haunted him ever since. And trying to avoid her every time he'd visited his foster mother hadn't helped the situation—it had only made it worse.

It had left him imagining he could almost catch the scent of Nell's subtly sexy perfume every time he'd visited. Until he'd found himself driving to City Hospital on the pretext of talking to her about Vivian.

Connor fought to shake off such uncharacteristic thoughts. But not before Vivian had noticed, her sharp gaze narrowing again.

'You seem preoccupied.'

'A case,' he answered smoothly, wiping the smile from his lips.

He might have known that she wouldn't fall for the lie.

'Is that so?' Her eyebrows shot up. 'And here I was thinking whoever she is might be why you were so reluctant to leave your current hospital.'

Vivian thought he'd been reluctant to leave his current post because of a woman? Connor sucked in an unimpressed breath even as a part of his brain argued that it was better for his foster mother to think that than have her realise that his unwelcome occupation lay much closer. Even so, he cast her a sharp glance.

'No one would come before you,' he told her gruffly. Hating the way her eyes looked so regretful.

'That isn't how it should be, Connor. If you truly believe that, then I failed in raising you.'

'You did not fail.' He couldn't accept that. 'You're the only reason I made it through. The only reason I didn't end up in some juvenile centre. Or worse, dead. I owe you everything, so trust me when I say that's exactly how it should be.'

'Why? Because you're afraid to ever open yourself up to anyone?'

'And offer them what?' He snorted scornfully. 'I'm damaged, Vivian. You know that better than most.'

'No.' Vivian refused to agree. 'I know your early childhood was hateful, Connor. One that no child should ever be subjected to. And I know you were wounded when you came to me—inside and out. But that never made you damaged beyond repair. You've worked so hard to heal yourself, and I'm so proud of everything you've achieved. But you deserve to sit back now and be loved, as well as to love in return.'

His chest tightened at her words, as though the weight of his past mistakes were sitting on his upper body, trying to suffocate him.

'I'm broken.' He gave a terse shake of his head.

'We both know it. I couldn't offer anyone anything but heartache.'

'Oh, Connor, I wish you could see the boy that I knew. I wish you realised the man you've become. You deserve to be happy and have everything that you want.'

'I do have everything I want,' he replied curtly. Automatically. Forcing a smile.

The saddest part was that a year ago he'd have said that was true—for the most part, at least. Though there was always that part of him that felt restless, always wanting to see what else was out there in the world. To experience something new. Something *more*.

It had been strange, coming in here the other night and seeing Ivan. He'd been steeling himself for seeing his foster mother, but he'd long since forgotten that there had been at least one other person who had made his time at Little Meadwood less… nightmarish.

It didn't matter, except that it had made him realise that amongst the hostility he remembered encountering in Little Meadwood as a kid, there had been at least one or two people besides his foster mother who had brought friendship and fun into his time here. He was beginning to realise he'd just buried those good moments along with all the bad ones.

And now, every time he tried to look at it, there was another piece of the jigsaw. A new piece that had no image yet, except its silhouette that looked suspiciously like a certain doctor.

It was nonsensical.

Vivian regarded him searchingly for a few moments.

'I want to see you happy before I die. I want to see all of you happy.'

A band pulled tight around his chest. How could he refuse to answer her now?

'What if I'm perfectly content with the way my life is?'

'You're not content.' Her voice was still soft, but firm. 'You're just afraid to take a chance. To risk getting hurt.'

'I'm not afraid of getting close to anyone. There has just never been anyone I would *want* to get close to in that way.'

Yet even as he spoke the words he knew they were a lie. Still, he pushed away the image of the blonde-haired doctor that had sprung straight into his mind.

Vivian's eyes raked sadly over his face.

'You don't have to live your life alone, Connor. You deserve love. Someone who loves you the way my Albert loved me.'

'That's easy for you to say.' He knew that she meant well, but he couldn't keep that tinge of bitterness and self-recrimination from creeping into his voice. 'You've always seen the best in people, including me—especially me.'

'And look at everything you've achieved for yourself. You're a surgeon, a war hero, and essentially a loving son.'

A son?

He wanted to speak but his throat felt suddenly thick. Tight.

'I know what your early childhood was like,' Vivian continued regardless. 'And I've seen the scars it has left on you—I've always known that they wouldn't disappear overnight. But that doesn't mean you have to let them define you. You seem different now from the last time I saw you, what was it…four years ago, now? Touring those pyramids at Giza that I'd never imagined I would ever see in person.'

She stopped, the warm memory lighting up her taut face, her watery eyes. He smiled in response.

'That was a good week,' he agreed.

'It was. And we had a blast. But you seem different even since then, Connor. Less…dissonant with yourself. Perhaps now is the time to create a new life for yourself? One that's filled with love and happiness.'

The silence swirled around them. Perhaps a minute passed, perhaps an hour. Connor opened his mouth to object, then closed it again, then opened it again.

Was Vivian right? He wanted to say not, but a year ago nothing—not even Vivian's illness—could have dragged him back to this place. *Meadwood.*

Yet visiting these past couple of weeks hadn't quite been the unbearable hell he'd imagined it would be.

Because being back in Meadwood was having more of an impact on him than he had cared to admit?

Or because someone *was?*

'But you still haven't discovered what it is you've spent the past two decades looking for.'

Connor's smile faded, replaced by a furrow of consternation.

'What makes you think that?' he asked quietly.

Vivian's eyes seemed to bore into his very soul as she regarded him.

'You're a gifted surgeon, dear. But there's more to life than just your work.'

Connor shifted uneasily in his seat, feeling the weight of her words bearing down on him. It was true that he'd always been driven by the need to excel in his career, to push himself to the limits of his abilities. But recently he'd also found himself questioning whether there was more to life than the relentless pursuit of success.

Nothing to do with Nell Parker, of course. It was just that her obvious contentment in staying in Meadwood seemed to have got under his skin in a way that he couldn't explain. Which had to be why it was her silhouette he saw.

'What if I don't know what I'm looking for?' he admitted, his voice low and uncertain.

Vivian leaned forward, placing her hand on his in a comforting gesture despite her tiredness.

'That's okay, dear, we can change the subject if you prefer. Just remember that sometimes it's enough to be open to the possibilities that life presents to us.'

'I remember,' he managed, determinedly thrusting any further images of Nell out of his mind.

'Like I said, I just want you to be happy.'

'I *am* happy,' he echoed.

'I'm sure you are.' Her voice was even softer. Almost…sad. 'But I worry that you could be happier. If only you'd just…let yourself be.'

'Happier how?' Even as he answered, he tried to swallow the words back.

Engaging with Vivian would only convince her that she was right. He should have just brushed her words off.

So why hadn't he?

'You could try settling down. Maybe not here, as much as I'd love it if you wanted that.' Vivian gripped his hand tighter, her bony fingers surprisingly strong as they bit into his skin. 'But somewhere you could call home.'

Home? The very word nearly made him scoff aloud. He wasn't sure how he managed to contain it.

'You could have a family, Connor,' Vivian continued urgently when he didn't answer.

This time there was no biting back the scornful response.

'*A family?* You and I both know that's the last thing I should ever do.'

'Because you have some foolish notion that since the man who sired you was no kind of father, then you would be the same?' Vivian challenged evenly.

'That,' he agreed caustically, 'and the fact that my so-called mother left me half feral. Evidently, it's in my blood.'

'That's utter nonsense, Connor, my boy.' And he couldn't decide whether his foster mother was more sad or cross. 'You're nothing like her. You're nothing like either of them. But you can't keep running from your past for ever. That won't make that hollowness inside you go away. It's time for you to start building a future for yourself.'

He gritted his teeth, wanting to refute her words There was always that *thing* inside him pushing him on, as if he was constantly searching for something to fill that empty space inside him that he couldn't quite name.

'This isn't a conversation I want to have right now,' he managed instead.

'Perhaps not.' Vivian shook her head tiredly. 'But if not now, then when? My time is clearly running out.'

Connor fell silent, not wanting to argue with her—and, worse, fighting that sliver inside him that seemed to want so desperately to believe what she was saying.

He *had* changed. When he'd walked away from

Little Meadwood twenty years ago, he'd sworn nothing would ever, ever bring him back. He'd still held onto that ten years ago. Even a year ago.

But these past twelve months…he'd felt something shifting in him, even if he'd refused to acknowledge it at the time. Ever since that UN peacekeeper deployment that had turned into such a nightmare.

Even now, some nights, in those hazy moments between wake and sleep he could still hear the laughter and life of that small village by the wadi. And then sleep would bring the horror. And the sheer sense of helplessness when his unit had returned to find the entire village razed to the ground. The thunderous silence of innocent villagers who had all paid the ultimate price simply for accepting much-needed medical aid from the so-called enemy.

His shift in mindset had begun after that. But was it possible he was really so different now? That maybe opening his life to someone wouldn't be such a terrible thing, after all. That maybe he could have something to offer…if it was the right woman. Though he resolutely refused to allow that image of a certain blonde-haired doctor to lurk around the edges of his brain. That was just an inconvenient attraction. Nothing more.

He eyed his foster mother, as if it were her fault he suddenly couldn't control his thoughts, even as the silence hung between them for several more long, telling moments.

'Cup of tea?' He finally changed the subject instead.

'If you'd prefer.' She inclined her head knowingly.

He would prefer. Because it didn't make sense to dwell on his new colleague. He was here for Vivian, not to indulge in some dalliance—and he got the impression that dalliances weren't Nell Parker's style.

Heading out to the compact kitchen, he busied himself with the drinks and by the time he returned to the living room, he was confident that his head was back where it should be.

'I hear you received an MBE for fostering. You never said.'

She didn't look the slightest bit chagrined. Instead, she eyed him shrewdly.

'Who told you that? Nell, or Ruby?'

Too late, he realised his mistake. Vivian was too sharp to miss a thing. He had no choice but to brazen it out.

'I wanted to know how you were really doing rather than the "nothing wrong with me" line that you keep giving me.'

'I'm going to guess Nell,' Vivian concluded, and he still couldn't lie.

Not to Vivian. She'd always been able to tell if he was lying, from when he was a mere kid.

'We ended up grabbing lunch,' he confessed as casually as he could, but he knew Vivian saw straight through it. Straight to things he wasn't even sure he could see himself.

Such as why he was so drawn to Nell.

Sure, she was beautiful with her swinging blonde hair and bright blue eyes, but he'd dated other beautiful women. Nell had more about her than just that. It was the way she carried herself, the way she spoke with authority and confidence, and yet had a kindness in her that seemed rare in the medical field. He found himself wanting to get to know her better, to learn more about what made her tick.

'Nell is a sweet girl,' Vivian said, perhaps a little too carefully.

Connor nodded, but didn't respond.

'Intelligent, and ambitious, too,' his former foster mum continued at length. 'Like you.'

'Why do I feel you're not precisely complimenting me?' he offered dryly.

'Do you need me to compliment you?'

It was an honest question, despite the light-hearted tone. Vivian had always had a knack for offering advice and guidance when it seemed as though he needed it most. Even now he couldn't deny that her words had a certain resonance that spoke of her deep personal concern for him. He felt touched by the gesture.

'No,' he replied finally with a slight smile. 'I don't need compliments.'

A slight smile tugged at her lips as she reached

up and patted his hand. 'I'm glad you're here, Connor. I've missed you.'

There was no swallowing the lump in his throat as Connor felt an inexplicable wave of...something he couldn't describe. Or didn't want to.

He turned his head as if that would help. Outside, the late evening light was finally beginning to dim, causing him to launch to his feet.

'I hadn't realised it was getting so late,' he rasped. 'You need to get your rest.'

'I was thinking the same about you,' Vivian noted, ever the maternal figure. 'Where are you staying? Not in a hotel?'

'No,' he answered quickly. Simply.

'Hospital accommodation, then?'

'A new on-site block,' Connor confirmed, deliberately declining to mention the sensor alarm issue.

He might have known he wouldn't get away with it.

'You're going to try to sleep through the intermittent alarm on some oversensitive sensor system?'

'How could you possibly have heard about that?' Connor rumbled, half amused, half incredulous. But Vivian's expression caused something to hitch in his chest. 'Ah. It was Nell, wasn't it? She shouldn't have worried you.'

'She didn't worry me,' Vivian denied firmly. 'It was just that she left me a garbled message earlier about some alarm fault at the hospital. I thought she'd misdialled but when I tried to call her back she was clearly tied up with patients. But she offered to let you stay at the cottage, didn't she?'

He should have taken a bet on Vivian being able to deduce that.

'How could you guess?'

'Because an hour or so later she sent me a text to say that she thought she would have to stay late to cover the next shift and to remind me where the spare key is *should I need it*.' Vivian shrugged lightly. 'I thought it was rather strange at the time. I worried she thought I was going a bit senile. Now I understand it.'

'She wouldn't dare think you're senile.' Connor couldn't help but laugh. 'None of us would.'

His foster mother chuckled.

'You better hadn't. Now, in the drawer of that white unit over there you'll find the keys to Nell's cottage.'

'Thanks—' he shook his head '—but I'm not staying there.'

Although the thought that Nell didn't expect to return tonight did cause him to waver.

Or he told himself that was what it was, anyway.

'You should reconsider.' Vivian seemed to read him too easily. 'If only for tonight. The sofa pulls out into a bed and the girls keep fresh sheets in the airing cupboard at the top of the stairs.'

'It's okay, the hospital admin have offered a hotel. I wouldn't want to inconvenience anyone. I'm fine.'

He'd had to stay awake for days in various theatres of war.

'I'm sure you think that's true, but there's no point martyring yourself if you can't get any sleep,' she clipped out briskly. 'I know how you feel about hotels, Connor, and if Nell's on duty then she won't be there anyway. Like I said—'

'*You're fine.* Yes, I heard. Shame those stifled yawns don't exactly instil confidence.'

As much as he didn't want to admit it, Vivian had a point. As had Nell. So why did the prospect of spending the night in the latter's cottage—even alone—leave his mouth feeling oddly dry?

As though there was something unsettling about the idea of staying in Nell's home. At least, he told himself that what he was feeling was *unsettled.* He refused to allow himself to think it was anything else. Certainly not something that would risk further complicating this strange, unexpected draw between him and Nell.

But the idea of staying close to his foster mother tonight was particularly reassuring. Especially since it appeared Nell, Ruby and Ivan were all out of the village. Plus, Nell *had* offered him her couch. And at least she wouldn't be there tonight.

'Fine.' He dipped his head. 'I'll stay. If only to be on hand should you need anyone.'

It was only when his foster mother offered a weary smile that he realised how exhausted she must be.

'I'd like that. Just take it easy and get some rest.'

'I could say the same.' He stepped forward to help her up out of her chair. 'Right, let me help you upstairs, and then I'll pop back down and clear up our things so you won't be waking up to a mess in the morning.'

Because it was better to keep busy than to dwell on thoughts of Nell Parker, instead.

CHAPTER SIX

As Nell pulled her car into the driveway, she was surprised to see the light on in the front room. She had expected it to be in darkness when she returned home. Nell had barely got out of the car when she spotted something else out of place. A large motorbike leaning against the drystone wall, silhouetted against the soft glow coming from the street lamp nearby.

Connor!

Her heart thudded abruptly as wild thoughts tumbled through her head.

Had he actually taken her up on her offer of crashing on her couch?

She shook her head, trying to stop herself from reading too much into it—it was only that she'd been convinced that, even with the issue of the faulty smoke-detection sensors in the surgeons' accommodation, Connor had been too proud to accept her offer.

It felt significant that he was here now. As though he trusted her in a way he evidently usually found hard to do.

Nell shook off those thoughts too, and instead headed towards the house. She paused just before stepping over the threshold, uncertain of what might come next when she opened her front door and stepped into a world that seemed to be getting ever more unpredictable by the hour.

And then she chastised herself for being ridiculous before pushing open the door and edging inside. She was met by silence as she moved down the hallway and to her living room, which now felt oddly unfamiliar to her, but even so she smoothed her expression into a neutral one before she rounded the corner.

She needn't have worried. Connor had obviously fallen asleep where he sat, his head resting back against the arm of the sofa with his hands crossed together over his bare chest—a breath-stealing sight—and that was even before her eyes settled on that faint quirk of a smile playing across his lips, as if he knew some secret joke only he was aware of.

Nell couldn't quite explain why, but something about the scene in front of her commanded her attention. She found herself moving closer and closer to Connor's sleeping form until she was standing right beside him. Her hand reached hesitantly forward, as if it weren't even under her control, and brushed a stray lock away from his forehead.

The contact was gentle yet jolting; a strange mix of electricity and warmth that thrummed through Nell like a current. But then Connor stirred and it was all she could do to leap away, as if she'd just been shocked.

By the time he sat up, instantly alert, she was turning her back to him and hanging her coat over the chair. Then again, that chiselled chest wasn't exactly helping her to stay focused.

Her heart pounded louder. Her palms actually itching with the ridiculous desire to reach out to him again.

It really ought to be a crime for any one man to be so tempting.

'I didn't mean to disturb you.' She had no idea how she managed to keep her voice so even.

'What time is it?' He reached for his watch, his voice entirely too gravelly, and sexy. And *just woken up*. Even when he let out a low curse. 'Just after one-thirty. Sorry, I understood from Vivian that you would be working the night shift. I never would have presumed…'

'It's fine, really. You didn't presume.' She couldn't stop a smile from quirking up the corners of her mouth. This was probably the closest this man ever came to being flustered. 'It isn't a problem at all, or else I wouldn't have offered in the first instance. And I *was* staying to cover the night shift after a multi-vehicle RTA on the main city road, and due to roadworks between us and City General, all the casualties had to be brought to us. It was mayhem so about five of us stayed on.'

'I was on duty, too, but I wasn't paged.' He didn't look pleased, though his gruff tone vibrated deliciously through her all the same.

'No, I think they were trying to give the surgeons from the third floor the night to sleep in peace.' Nell lifted her shoulders slightly.

'Ah, that makes sense. You were right about the smoke-sensor issue,' he confirmed. 'The hospital admin chief contacted me about an hour after you'd told me and assured me she'd secured courtesy hotel rooms for all affected, but I was here visiting Vivian this evening, and I thought I'd stick around to take her to breakfast tomorrow.'

'She'll love that.' Nell fumbled in her bag, as much for something to occupy her shaking hands as anything else.

'Okay, then.'

'And, as I mentioned, Ruby won't mind you crashing here either.' As if mentioning her flatmate could somehow make this moment feel even marginally less intimate. She was sure she wasn't just imagining it. 'She has gone away for a few days.'

'Apparently so has Ivan.'

'Ivan has?' She jerked her head up, suddenly curious.

Why couldn't she shake the idea that there was something going on between Ivan and her friend? But surely Ruby would have mentioned it? They'd always told each other everything, ever since they were kids.

Connor didn't exactly shrug, but there was a slight hint of a broad, muscled shoulder.

'I get the impression that whatever is going on with Ruby includes him.'

'I thought I was imagining things.' Nell gave a half-embarrassed laugh, heat stealing into her cheeks.

Connor grinned, his eyes glinting with amusement.

'Believe me, you're not imagining anything. There's a definite attraction.'

He stopped abruptly, right at the moment Nell felt herself freeze. And though he didn't move even an inch, it felt as though he had as something had shifted right there in the room. It made the air heavier, closer…and infinitely more intimate. She was painfully aware of her breath coming out faster than it should. Her very skin vibrating with awareness of him. The scent of freshly showered skin that seemed to fill up the space between them. Were they still talking about Ruby and Ivan? She wasn't sure. When was the last time she'd ever felt so flustered around a man? Especially one who was currently occupying her living room.

And still they each stared at the other as the night silence suddenly seemed to weave itself around them. Nell, breath caught in her throat, was desperate to break the moment before its intensity became too much for either of them to bear. She opened her mouth with no idea what she might say, only for Connor to beat her to it, his voice low and husky again.

'Anyway, I should probably get a drink and let you get some sleep.'

Nell nodded, feeling a strange mix of disappointment and relief. She was beginning not to trust herself to be alone with Connor for much longer without doing something she might regret. It was a novel notion for her. When had any man ever got under her skin quite like Connor? Even Jonathon?

She moved to leave the room, then paused at the door.

'Oh, just thought you might be interested to know that after our conversation today I asked my patient where she had been and discovered it had been on the same street as my first patient. Then I checked her for needle marks.'

'You found them,' he said flatly, reading her face.

'On her backside, just like you said,' Nell confirmed. 'Obviously, I can't check the girl from the weekend before, but I remember her thinking she had a bite in the same location, and the itch was driving her mad. I checked it and it was a little bit raised and red but I wasn't looking for a needle mark back then. Now I can't help wondering.'

'They aren't easy to spot, especially if you aren't expecting to see anything like that. Did you tell your current patient to contact the police?'

'I did,' she confirmed. 'They came and took a statement, and when I mentioned about the first girl they said they would contact her and ask if she would be happy to give her story to see if there were any similarities that could help.'

'Not an easy conversation—' he held her gaze '—but better than them wandering around in the dark.'

Nell nodded.

'Bizarrely, I think it helped, in a way. I know both girls felt under pressure from others—one from her sister, the other from her parents—to admit they'd had too much to drink, yet both girls were adamant that they hadn't. I guess this possibility allows them to trust their own convictions. Although now I guess they have a whole other set of issues to try to wrap their heads around.'

'The worst of it is that we're seeing more and more of these cases coming into hospitals.'

She shook her head trying to clear it of the shock of the evening.

'Anyway, thanks again for the pointer. I never would have thought to look for a needle mark, otherwise. Goodnight, Connor.'

'Goodnight, Nell.'

He stretched, and stood, causing his muscles to ripple. Nell swallowed hard, looking away. But it was too late, and the image was already burned wickedly into her mind. All she could do was attempt to ignore the way her body was reacting to him. At least he was wearing jogging bottoms. She wasn't sure she'd have coped if he'd just been in boxers. But as he made his way towards the kitchen door, Nell couldn't help but feel a sense of…loss? Longing? She wasn't sure what it was, but it was a feeling she hadn't experienced in a long time. Maybe it was just the fact that she was tired, and her emotions were all over the place. Or maybe it was something more.

As he disappeared into the kitchen, her shaky legs carried her upstairs and into her bedroom where she collapsed on her bed with a shaky breath.

Her mind raced with thoughts she had no chance of quelling—not the least of which was the fact that she'd fled upstairs so hastily that she hadn't even had the coffee she'd been longing for all evening.

Connor's presence in her small cottage was intoxicating. As much as she'd tried before, it was now impossible to deny just how much she wanted him. Like some hormonal adolescent. Laughable really, since she'd never been like that even when she *had* been that age. Yet here she was, barely able to think straight. Obsessing over the man downstairs, cloistered in her room as she listened out for his footfalls that would tell her when he left the kitchen and headed back to the couch.

Clearly having Connor in her house, even just for the night, was going to be a challenge—one that she wasn't sure she was ready for.

So would she have preferred he hadn't taken her up on her offer?

Nell eyed her reflection in the mirror, as if she could somehow be more honest with the person she saw there. The inconvenient truth was that there was something about Connor Mason that made her feel alive in a way that she hadn't felt for a very long time. Perhaps ever. Even Jonathon had never made her feel so...*electric*. He had never looked at her with eyes so piercing that it seemed as though they saw right into her soul. He had never made her feel as if she were the only woman in the room, even when it was crowded.

But Connor had—which made him dangerous and thrilling all at the same time.

What would it be like to be with a man like him? To feel his strong arms around her, kiss those sinful lips, and run her fingers through hair that looked as though it was artfully tousled even when he'd hauled off his motorbike helmet after a long ride? Lord, but he was all so tempting, so enticing. And yet also so terrifying.

The woman reflected in the mirror blew out an exasperated sigh and rolled her eyes. Then, with a deep breath, Nell crossed her room and yanked the door open with a decisiveness that she didn't entirely feel, and ultimately made her way back down the stairs. As she entered the kitchen, she found Connor pouring himself another glass of water. He looked up when he heard her footsteps, and their eyes met once again.

'I know it's late and I'll probably never sleep but I've spent the past few hours on shift just dreaming of a decent, non-vending-machine coffee.' She forced a light laugh as she busied herself with the kettle and mug, her hand hovering over a second cup. 'Would you like one?'

There was the briefest beat of hesitation before he nodded once.

'Sure, why not?' Stepping beside her, he took the mugs from her hand and reached for the labelled coffee jar on the shelf. 'I'll make it whilst you sit down—you're the one who has just come off shift.'

'Oh…right…' Surprised, and more than a little gratified, Nell allowed him to take over. 'Thanks.'

It was such a small gesture that nonetheless made her feel curiously valued. She couldn't help smiling inside as he moved around her kitchen, his movements purposeful and efficient, murmuring her thanks as he held out the hot mug for her to take. And there was no denying that frisson that shot up her arm and around her whole being when their fingers brushed for that fraction of a moment. An unintended slip that felt ridiculously intimate.

Focus on the coffee.

Lifting the steaming mug to her lips, Nell inhaled the rich aroma before taking a tentative but appreciate sip.

'So good,' she managed, before taking another.

'Long shift,' he empathised.

'Very.' She twisted her mouth up. 'And a difficult one.'

He leaned back on the kitchen counter, his eyes fixed on hers.

'The nightclub case still getting to you? Want to talk?' he asked simply. Quietly.

As if he could read her every thought, making her feel exposed. Vulnerable.

Still, she forced herself to meet his gaze.

'Actually, the case really getting to me was a pregnant woman in that RTA. Neither of them made it.'

'Ah.' Connor nodded. 'That must have been a hard case.'

'Yeah.' She squeezed her eyes closed for a second. 'I can usually switch off to the trauma of it, and just do the absolute best job I can for my patients.' She shrugged. 'But tonight just got to me. It felt like such a kick in the gut. The loss… I don't know.'

'You're carrying around the worry of Vivian right now.' He reached out and placed a comforting hand on her shoulder—a simple movement, but it sent delicious shivers down Nell's spine.

It was all she could do not to topple sideways off her stool.

'Shall we go through?' she managed, jerking her head to the living room instead.

It was only when she stepped through the doorway that she saw that he'd set up his bed on the couch. At least the room was bigger than the kitchen though; moving to the furthest corner, Nell sank down in the oversized tub chair and folded her legs up underneath her. She wasn't sure whether to feel gratified or disappointed when he reached down to snag a black T-shirt from his bag and haul it over his head.

'I'll be out of your way in a minute or two,' she promised, taking another sip of gloriously hot coffee.

'Take your time.' Connor's voice rasped through the air. 'I'm probably up for a couple of hours now anyway. If you're hungry I could make us something to eat. What have you got in?'

Nell pulled a sheepish face.

'Porridge oats, bread, and couple of chocolate snack bars if we're lucky.'

'That's it?' He looked incredulous.

'Well, there are probably a few other ingredients out there—every so often Ruby and I decide we'll make something exciting, but then work gets in the way and we usually grab something on the way home from the hospital.'

Glancing at his watch, Connor stood up abruptly.

'Where's the nearest supermarket? I can probably grab us something decent.'

She pulled another face—this time more apologetic, despite her amusement.

'This is Meadwood, not the city. We don't have twenty-four-seven supermarkets, just Sylvie's corner shop, which will have closed hours ago.'

She was sure she caught the hint of an odd expression ripple across his face.

'How do you survive out here?' he muttered, his

eyes scanning the room as if searching for a stash of hidden food.

'We manage.' Nell laughed, her spirits lifting in spite of everything.

'Well, that's not going to work,' he grumbled, running a hand through his tousled hair. 'I guess we'll just have to make do with what we've got. I'll see what I can rustle up.'

Nell watched him move back to the kitchen, and found herself following. He rummaged through her cupboards and fridge with a practised ease and she couldn't help but feel a little envious of his confidence in the kitchen.

'Breakfast or supper?'

'Supper,' she confirmed definitively.

'Okay…hmm…peppers, rice, onions, tomatoes. Have you any chicken broth…? Yes. Great. How about spicy Mexican rice?'

Her stomach rumbled obligingly.

'Sounds good,' she admitted.

'Okay.' He picked up a pan from the rack and began to fill it. 'I'll get the rice on, the broth, and then chop the onions. You chop the peppers.'

'That I can manage,' she agreed, leaning over to tap the small speaker on the side. 'Might as well have a little background music whilst we work.'

'Even better.'

Whilst he quickly measured out the rice by eye, she set to work retrieving half-decent knives from the drawer for each of them, then chopping the pepper. But Nell still couldn't stop her eyes from wandering over to study this man of such contradictions.

Even dressed in just a black T-shirt and joggers, he really was devastatingly handsome. She tried to push the thought out of her mind. It was dangerous to think of him like that—just as it was hard to remember that, despite the fact that Vivian had mentioned Connor for as long as Nell had known her, she herself had met the man only recently.

It felt like longer—and in a good way.

So as she took in the way his muscles moved under his shirt and the way his hair fell across his forehead that low, familiar ache crept back into her belly. It had been so long since she had been with anyone, let alone someone like him.

As if sensing her gaze, he turned to her with a half-smile.

'You know, you're pretty good company for someone who's exhausted and just had a rough shift,' he said, handing her a couple of tomatoes.

Nell grinned despite herself, a warm flush spreading across her cheeks.

'You're not so bad yourself.'

They fell into a comfortable silence as they prepped, the only sounds coming from their rhythmic chopping, and the speaker playing in the background. Cutting and dicing, then sliding the ingredients into a bowl whilst Connor moved around her kitchen as though he were utterly familiar with

the set-up—as though he *belonged*—and worked on everything else.

Before long, the mouth-watering smells of the rice dish filled the kitchen and Nell's stomach began to growl louder in appreciation.

Connor ladled out two generous helpings onto plates and they sat together at the counter, their conversation flowing easily as they ate. And even when they had finished, they chatted for a little longer before reluctantly beginning to clean up and load the mini-dishwasher. Taking more time than they needed. Finding extra little tasks. It seemed that neither of them felt any desire to break the spell that had been cast over them.

And then the song on the speaker changed to something slow, and soft, and the atmosphere in the room shifted again. Nell couldn't stop her gaze from being drawn once more to Connor's, only to find him looking back intently.

'Wait, you have…' He reached out and brushed a stray pepper seed off her cheek, his mouth curved into a soft smile. His eyes lingering on hers for a moment too long.

Without thinking, Nell took a step closer until she was standing mere inches from him, revelling in the way his eyes dropped to her mouth when she flicked a nervous tongue over her suddenly dry lips. A thousand thoughts spun wildly through her head.

Did she say something? Move away?

Her heart fluttered even as her lungs appeared

to momentarily forget what they had been doing—without issue—for over three decades. And then, almost without warning, Connor bent his head down and lightly brushed his lips against hers.

And it was as though the spark it ignited in Nell somehow both silenced those tumbling thoughts and sent them crazy all at the same time. She melted into the kiss, basking in the rush of exhilaration that cascaded through her body. And when his arms came around her waist to pull her closer, Nell was helpless to do anything but slide her hands up that gloriously solid chest of his to loop her arms around his neck.

It was everything she had been pretending not to dream about—and so, so much more.

He deepened the kiss, his hands moving to cup her face as though she were infinitely precious. Undisguised hunger. Demanding...*taking*. Every delicious sweep of his tongue against her lips made Nell shiver with delight. Every new sensation that he created sent electricity coursing through her veins. It was as if time had paused, leaving nothing else but the two of them and the heat between them. Every fresh touch sent a wave of heat through her body, igniting a fire that had been dormant for far too long.

Nell's hands roamed eagerly over Connor's body, savouring every detail as she mapped out the hardness of his muscles beneath his shirt. Down further, to where his shirt ended and his skin began. He had ignited a veritable fire in her belly just as he had infused molten lava into her very veins. It grew hot-

ter and brighter with each movement of his hands, and still she couldn't get enough. She was addicted to his touch.

Could he feel the shake of barely controlled desire in her hands as she traced the delicious contours of his chest? Mapping them. Committing them to memory. And still his mouth demanded from hers—*took* from hers—whilst his hands sought out her waist, slipping underneath her shirt to tease her flesh into writhing pleasure. A strangled moan escaped Nell's throat as he explored further, a maddening desire filling her from the tips of her toes, right up. And when he finally dragged his mouth from hers, he lifted her off the ground and placed her onto the counter but still didn't release her. Not that she wanted him to release her.

Ever.

She pushed that thought away, instead concentrating on tracing the contours of his abs, feeling the hardness of his muscles and the warmth of his skin. The next kiss that was every bit as hot and intense as the last. His tongue exploring her mouth with just the right amount of pressure, her head cradled in his hand. Pleasure and need consumed Nell; a need that was as vital as breathing, too strong to contain. Her heart was beating so fast in her chest, she wondered if he could feel it. If this was what it felt like to be in a bubble suspended in time, and in the perfect moment, then she wanted it never to burst.

Connor broke the kiss to bury his face in her

neck, his breath hot against her skin as he nipped at the sensitive flesh. Dimly, she heard a soft moan that surely wasn't her. It was as if her mind were hazy and yet flawlessly clear all at once. His hands roamed beneath her shirt to caress her breasts. She gasped at the sensation, arching into his touch.

He looked up at her through eyes so dark. As if he was as lost as she was. Like nothing she'd ever quite experienced before.

Did she drive him as crazy as he drove her? Dimly, Nell could only hope so, if this desperate, primal kiss was anything to go by. A promise of what was to come. And it set every nerve-ending firing inside her.

The shrill sound of a mobile phone caught them both off guard, ripping through the air. Making them pull apart.

She couldn't help wondering if he was being battered by the same storm of stupefaction, and frustration, and regret, that was battering through her.

'It's Vivian's ringtone,' he rasped sharply, spinning from her and striding back into the living room.

Leaving her to slide down from the counter herself, her arms wrapped around her chest, heart still hammering, though for a different reason now.

'Is she okay?' Nell asked, though she knew he couldn't possibly know.

Her teeth worried at her lower lip as Connor slid his finger over the screen to accept the call.

'Vivian? What's wrong?'

Unable to hear the other side of the conversation, Nell hovered anxiously by the door, her arms still hugging herself protectively. She didn't want to just burst in next door if it wasn't serious, so all she could do was watch Connor's face carefully as she fought to control her lurching heart.

And then he looked up at her, meeting her gaze for a long moment.

'I'm fine, Vivian. I'm next door…at Nell and Ruby's. You gave me your spare key, do you remember?'

The tension in Nell's chest dropped instantly to the ground as her knees threatened to buckle.

Her foster mum was okay.

Another few reassuring words from Connor, and then he was ending the call, apologising again. He tossed the phone down to the sofa bed, his arms folding across his chest as he faced her.

But he didn't close the gap, and his expression was frustratingly impossible to read.

'She was calling to make sure I was safely back home. I usually call her to say I've arrived safely.'

'She hadn't realised you were here, then?' Nell asked, redundantly.

'I did tell her that I would be but I'm guessing that the meds she's on have disorientated her, especially as she had just woken.' He stopped, fixing Nell with a piercing gaze. 'She told me you had called her to remind her where the spare key was, right before she persuaded me that crashing here would be the wisest option.'

His considered tone didn't stop her heart from skipping a beat or two.

'Well…yes, I did do that.' Nell's mouth was dry and it was all she could do not to lick her lips. 'Was she alright when you reminded her? Did she remember?'

'She did,' Connor confirmed. 'She was a little cross with herself for forgetting but I think I reassured her that it didn't matter.'

'Okay, good. Then I'm just thankful she's well and there isn't an issue.'

'Right,' he agreed, his voice sounding as stilted as hers.

'I should…that is… I'd better head to bed,' she managed to stutter out.

As if her head and heart weren't still reeling. Still wanting more.

'Probably for the best,' he concurred, his voice taut. 'Goodnight, Nell.'

'Night,' she managed before fleeing upstairs to bed.

Not that she stood a hope in hell of getting a wink of sleep.

CHAPTER SEVEN

'HEY, CONNOR, any update yet?'

Connor barely lifted his head as the surgical head of trauma ducked into his operating room, instead keeping his attention on the patient in front of him.

'Just getting into the wound now,' he confirmed. 'Give me a moment.'

He worked quickly but carefully, grateful as ever for the surgical work to keep his mind busy and off a certain blonde-haired temptress.

It had been three days since that night at Nell's cottage in Meadwood. Four nights since he'd almost forgotten himself completely.

He knew he owed her an apology but he hadn't been able to trust himself enough to return to her home once he'd left the following morning. He was only grateful the contractors had remedied the smoke-sensor system so quickly, but he would have taken a night of intermittent alarm calls over returning to Nell's cottage.

As it was, it had taken all he had not to stop her from leaving the kitchen that night. To stop her from racing upstairs—away from him. As if distancing themselves from each other could extinguish the spark of attraction he felt to her.

Not that it had worked.

Thoughts of Nell kept flooding his brain every time he left it unoccupied—it didn't matter how strenuously he tried to deny replaying that night over in his head, or how vehemently he told himself that he didn't remember how it felt to kiss her, or even how staunchly he pretended not to recall the way her hands had so willingly explored his body in a way that still sent lingering waves of heat through him.

No matter what he told himself, Connor couldn't pretend that he'd imagined that pull between them—even from the first moment they'd met at the site of Lester's car crash—or tell himself over and over that it was simply a connection due to the fact that they'd both been foster kids under Vivian's care. Deep down Connor knew there was more than that.

But he couldn't allow himself to give into it. A woman like Nell deserved better than a man like him. Better than a meaningless one-night stand—because that was all he could offer her.

And no matter that a part of him imagined what it might be like if he had more to give.

He shoved the uninvited thought from his mind and focused back in on his patient.

'The pole ultimately created a seven-inch slash across the abdomen,' Connor confirmed to his colleague, carefully walking his fingers around the inside of the cavity. Feeling his way and checking. Then checking again. 'But the good news is that the wound doesn't appear to penetrate beyond the anterior wall.'

'That is good,' his chief agreed, peering over the table from as far back as he could. 'So no damage to either the spleen or liver after all?'

'No.' Connor continued probing, concentrating on anything that might get his attention. The spleen and liver were the organs most often damaged in these types of injuries, followed by the retroperitoneum, small bowel and kidneys. Nothing here looked out of place. 'Plus the patient doesn't appear to have unexplained bleeding, vitals have been relatively stable, and there's no evidence of peritonitis. He had a FAST scan to assess for hemoperitoneum, and hemopericardium.'

'Good.'

The operating room fell into silence as Connor made another sweep of the wound before satisfying himself that nothing had been missed, then set to work as diligently and efficiently as ever. Because no matter the circumstances here, it was always better than the conditions he'd had to work in whilst on tours of duty. And he still missed that time of his life.

'Haemostasis?' the consultant asked, when Connor confirmed he was happy.

Connor nodded.

'Haemostasis also seems normal.'

'Lucky boy, then.'

'Very,' Connor confirmed.

The boy had been thrown through the windscreen of his car when he'd lost control on a tight bend and contact with a jagged metal pole had left him with a seven-inch long, somewhat deep slash across the left side of his abdomen. The fact that it hadn't penetrated into the body cavity and damaged the internal organs had been little short of a miracle.

The last similar case Connor had worked on back at his previous hospital, the man in question had ended up with a torn smaller intestine, which had resulted in significant resection. This boy by contrast had been very fortunate.

'We're going to start closing up now,' he updated the consultant, as he directed his fellow surgeon to where he wanted to start.

'Actually, if you can hand off for closing up, there's an emergency case downstairs right now that could really do with someone of your experience,' the chief told him.

'Of course.' Connor ignored the jolt that charged through him, like a thump from touching a live cable. 'I'll be right behind you.'

Was Nell on duty today?

He couldn't imagine she'd be delighted at being thrown together on a case—not after how they'd left things. But what choice was there? Besides, even if she was on shift, there were plenty of other doctors—and patients—who might need him. He was here for his patients—no one else.

Certainly not soft-lipped, hot-bodied Nell Parker.

And if he believed that, he'd believe anything.

Handing off to his colleague before stepping away from the table, Connor began stripping his gown and gloves and moving towards the sink area to scrub out.

Maybe moving to City Hospital hadn't been the wisest decision, after all—even if it did mean being closer to Vivian. Not to mention the fact that being so close to Little Meadwood was a little like taking twenty steps backwards into a past that hadn't exactly been fun the first time around.

He hadn't even begun to unpack that particular hang-up yet.

He hurried down the polished, pristine corridors around City Hospital's operating rooms—another reason to appreciate his new position at his new place of employment.

The recently refitted City Hospital was high-tech and bang up to date, with particularly forward-thinking surgeons. Despite his concerns about taking a job so close to Little Meadwood, Connor had to admit he was enjoying working in such an innovative environment.

Even the stairs were in a striking glass block that offered stunning views of the public park opposite, Connor thought as he raced down them three at a time, hurrying through the wide, quiet staff corridor and into the Resus department at the far end where his new boss was just concluding a conversation with another colleague.

'Connor.' His colleague peered around him. 'You're on your own?'

'Yes, where do you want me?'

With an appreciative nod, the consultant glanced at the digital board.

'Three cases but only two of us. The others must be on their way.' He grimaced. 'I'm about to take Bay Ten to emergency surgery, Bay Five is a blood clot on the chest, and Bay Eight is a fall due in. You'll need to assess both and identify priority.'

'Sure.' Connor dipped his head, sweeping the department quickly before heading over to Bay Eight.

'I'm Connor, the trauma surgeon you requested,' he announced as he stepped around the curtain. 'What have we got?'

And then he experienced the hardest wallop to his gut as Nell Parker spun around to meet his gaze, her familiar blue eyes stealing the breath from his lungs.

'Connor.'

Her sharp intake of breath told him everything he didn't want to admit he was thinking. He fought to regain control of his rattling senses.

'Nell,' he acknowledged briefly.

'I just didn't expect…' She faltered.

'Neither did I.' He cut her off, though not unkindly. 'How about you tell me about the case?'

She hesitated for another moment before bobbing her head quickly as he watched her professional side kick in.

Like him.

He pushed the comparison away—he didn't need another reason to suggest they were well matched.

'Patient is a twenty-six-year-old male who fell from an office roof and is complaining of lower back and pelvic pain,' Nell stated. 'He's with Heli-med, already landed and arriving any moment now and the only other information we have so far is that he had a GCS of fourteen when they arrived on scene, but there's been a period of hypotension.'

'Right.' Connor nodded grimly. 'After a fall like that, any hypotension would be consistent with pelvic injury and blood loss; possible spinal fractures; potential head injury...'

'Leading to something more serious,' Nell confirmed.

'Did you call anyone from Neurology?'

'I've alerted them.' She nodded.

'Good, I need to check on Bay Five, but I'll be back.'

Hurrying across the floor, he checked in on the other patient mentioned—a blood clot on the chest, which warranted surgery as advised, including deflating the lung to carry out the procedure. But he would need to wait for Nell's patient before determining which of them should take priority. He strode back to her bay just as the doors at the far end burst open and a Heli-med uniformed doctor hurried in with the gurney and she leapt into action.

'Bay Eight, please.'

Connor scanned everything at once as Nell began

the primary survey with her team—smooth and skilled. He found he expected nothing less from her, which helped him shove his own jumbled thoughts out of his head.

'Okay, IV in?' He checked with his team. 'Good. Can we get oxygen, please? And suction? Great.'

The process continued quickly and calmly with the team responding until they finally confirmed they were ready for the handover from the HEMS doctor, and Connor gave the man a nod.

'This is James, a twenty-six-year-old male who, approximately thirty minutes ago, fell around twenty-five feet off the roof of a small office block. He landed on his back and when we arrived, he had a GCS of fourteen and has been complaining of lumbar pain and pelvic pain. Top down, he has a laceration to the right frontal region of his head, lumbar pain and posterior pelvic pain, but was able to move his legs normally on scene. We've administered one hundred and fifty mil of ketamine to help control the pain.'

'Okay, thanks.' Connor took over from the Helimed team smoothly. 'Nell?'

He waited for her to confirm the checks with her team.

'Sounds equal airway bilaterally.' She nodded after a moment. 'No visible bruising to the chest. SATS ninety-eight. Good volume central pulse. Diminished volume peripheral pulse.'

Good. At least that could buy them a little time.

'Response?' he asked, but she was already on it.

'Hi, James, I'm Nell.' She kept her voice perfectly light and bright for the patient. 'Can you open your eyes for me? Great. And can you squeeze my hand? Good man.'

Connor dipped his head in confirmation when she glanced his way, before summoning her to one side.

'Can we get X-rays, please? Chest and pelvis,' Connor instructed. 'Can I leave this with you? I have to head to surgery with a patient with a blood clot on his chest. I'm going to have to collapse the lung and remove the clot via keyhole surgery.'

'Of course,' Nell confirmed. 'With any luck we'll have the results by the time you return.'

'Great.' He nodded.

Or else one of his colleagues should be arriving any moment.

And with that he was gone, leaving Nell to organise her team and get James the X-rays they needed—and leaving them both time to regroup.

'I've missed this,' Nell admitted as she and Ruby linked arms together and strolled through the park opposite the hospital. 'This morning was mayhem.'

For as long as she could recall, it had been their weekly ritual to take a walk around Little Meadwood and share any worries or concerns—or just fun stories—at least one day each week when they both had a day off.

How long had it been since they'd managed that?

Certainly not in the past few months—which only made Nell all the more grateful that her friend had found her on shift and asked if she'd like to meet up for a lunchbreak in the nearby park. Exactly what Nell had felt she needed after her morning with Connor—even if working alongside him kept proving surprisingly easy.

Given the tension between them after that night at her cottage, Nell certainly hadn't expected to share such a professional harmony and synchronicity with the man.

It made her wonder…

No! She slammed the thought away before it could take root inside her head.

But the fact was that by the time Connor had returned from his blood-clot surgery, they'd had the X-rays back on their patient, James, which had confirmed a pelvic fracture as well as indicating a strong possibility of spinal damage. Then together, they'd worked seamlessly to prep their patient for surgery, anticipating each other's needs as they'd stabilised his condition enough to get him to the OR. As though they'd been working together for years. She couldn't help feeling a sense of pride in their joint efforts.

But now…?

'Tell me about it.' Ruby rubbed one hand over her eyes, pulling Nell back to the present. 'I'm used to Resus being slammed but that was insane. I think there are still roadworks in the city so it has been quicker and easier to get all the emergencies here. And, for the record, I've missed this too.' Ruby squeezed Nell's arm in a show of affection. 'I'm sorry if I've been a bit distant recently.'

Nell bobbed her head. She couldn't pretend she hadn't noticed, especially with the jumble of Connor-related thoughts tumbling around her brain right now. But more than that, she and Ruby had been close for so many years that the sudden disconnect had worried her.

It had made her feel oddly isolated. Which had set other, unexpected questions firing off around her brain—such as what Little Meadwood would be like without either Vivian or Ruby around? It was something she'd never considered before.

Or never allowed herself to consider.

But that wasn't a scenario she was ready to dig into right now. She turned her attention back to her friend.

'Want to share?' she asked gently.

Ruby opened her mouth, then closed it before rubbing her hand over her eyes again.

'It's crazy. And complicated.'

'You don't have to feel obligated.' Nell stopped her friend instantly, but Ruby shook her head.

'I know. But… I want to. I just don't know where to start.'

Nell knew how her friend felt.

'Start wherever feels comfortable,' she suggested.

Perhaps she ought to take her own advice.

'It's just I've been…wondering about what it would be like to live somewhere else.'

'Oh.'

Was this something to do with Ivan? If so, why hadn't Ruby said something, anything, before now?

'Haven't you ever thought about leaving Meadwood?' Ruby asked as Nell pressed her lips together.

The question was all too close to the bone.

So much for not digging into that scenario.

'Not really,' she lied evenly.

As if the worry hadn't been there festering in the back of her mind.

'Never?' Ruby sounded sceptical and confused all at once, only adding to Nell's sense of guilt. 'What about with Jonathon?'

The feeling of guilt intensified. It occurred to her that she had never really explained to Ruby exactly why her engagement to him had unravelled. In fact, hadn't she revealed more to Connor than she ever had to her friend? So much for her telling herself that she and Ruby always told each other everything.

So what did that say about her?

'I don't really like thinking about what it might be like to stay here if Vivian…wasn't next door any more,' Nell finally offered as a compromise.

They both knew what she was trying not to say.

'Everywhere we went there would be memories,' Ruby conceded. 'Good ones but still…how could we walk past Vivian's house knowing that she wasn't there any longer?'

'Are you thinking about leaving?' Nell asked directly.

Ruby hesitated.

'Not now. Not unless…like I said, it's complicated.'

Their arms still linked, Nell led her friend to a wooden bench and they sank down next to each other.

'What's going on, Rubes? Only, you're right, you've been so preoccupied lately.' And the worst of it was that she herself had been so caught up with thoughts of Connor recently that it had taken her until now to notice that Ruby hadn't been herself for weeks. 'You know I'm always here for you to talk to.'

Ruby bobbed her head, leaning back. She was ostensibly taking in the warm rays of sunshine that filtered through the trees, but Nell suspected her friend was trying to work out what to say. It was so unlike Ruby that it caught in Nell's chest. They'd always told each other everything, right from being foster kids together. She hated that there were now secrets, that Ruby had things she couldn't share. But wasn't she just as bad?

Nell sucked in a deep breath.

'Okay, how about I go first? I kissed Connor.'

Ruby's head snapped around, her shock visible.

'Connor? As in *Connor Mason*?'

A nervous chuckle escaped Nell's throat.

'The very same. It happened the other night when you were away and he stayed at our cottage.'

'A kiss?'

'A good kiss.' Nell couldn't help grinning at the memory.

Ruby's eyebrows shot up.

'Wow, Nell. It's been ages since you even liked anyone enough to go on a date. Over a year, in fact. I didn't realise you had those kinds of feelings for Connor Mason.'

'I didn't either, to be honest,' Nell admitted. 'It's just...there's been something between us since that first time we met on the road after Lester's accident, you remember? This insane attraction... I can't explain it.'

'You don't have to, trust me.' Ruby's voice was odd. Not her usual light tone.

Nell reached out a hand to her friend's arm.

'Rubes?'

'Ignore me.' Ruby forced out a laugh. 'Long shift. So, have you talked to Connor since the kiss?'

Nell hesitated. She and Ruby had been friends long enough, and been through so much as foster kids together, that they could reach each other better than anyone. But it was clear that something more was going on with Ruby than she was ready to talk about. Even now her friend's gaze wasn't entirely focused; she was still partially lost in her own thoughts. Part of Nell ached to ask, to press her, yet the last thing Nell wanted to do was push her before she was ready. All she could do was make sure Ruby knew she was there to listen when her friend was ready.

Squeezing Ruby's hand, Nell plastered a rueful expression on her face.

'No, I haven't really had the chance to speak with Connor.'

Ruby wrinkled her nose thoughtfully.

'But you want to?'

'Yes. No. Maybe.' Nell shook her head with a strangled laugh, her eyes trained on some ducks across the old clay fields. 'I confess I haven't really had the courage. I think we sort of avoided each other for the rest of the time. But now I wish we hadn't. Sometimes I think there is a real connection there, but the reality is that we have nothing in common. I love Little Meadwood, he hates it. I worry that any connection we feel is actually just the shared experience of Vivian being ill.'

Ruby's gaze sharpened as she regarded her friend.

'I understand exactly what you mean,' she said, then trailed off. Once again as if there was something more she wanted to say, but couldn't.

Nell had to bite her own tongue to stop herself from prying.

When Ruby is ready, she reminded herself.

'I don't want to make things awkward with him,' she made herself say instead. 'Especially with everything going on with Vivian.'

'Sometimes it's hard to know what to do with those kinds of feelings,' Ruby demurred. 'But I think you have to be honest with yourself about what you feel. And what you want.'

And there was something about her friend's tone that made Nell wonder which of them Ruby was really trying to convince. Maybe letting her friend come to her in her own time was a good idea, but then maybe Ruby needed a gentle nudge. Didn't everyone, sometimes?

'Sounds like it makes sense,' Nell pointed out softly. 'Do you think you'll take your own advice, Rubes?'

Turning her head, Ruby met her gaze. There was a vulnerability in her friend's eyes that Nell couldn't help but respond to. Ruby's voice was quiet as she spoke, almost hesitant.

'I don't know, Nell. It's all so complicated.'

Nell reached out and squeezed Ruby's hand comfortingly.

'Whenever you're ready, Rubes. I'm here for you no matter what.'

Ruby's lips quirked up in a small smile, but there was still a sadness in her eyes that tugged at Nell's heartstrings.

'Thanks, Nell. I appreciate it.'

The two of them sat there in silence for a moment, lost in their own thoughts.

'Rubes...'

But whatever else Nell might have been about

to say was cut off as each of their phones shrieked alerts in quick succession. There was no need to read them to know what they would say.

'More emergencies.' The pair of them shared a look even as they turned and headed straight back to the hospital.

'One heck of a day.'

Connor's voice startled Nell as she snatched a couple of minutes to grab a coffee, after several hours of non-stop major emergencies.

She swung around, valiantly trying to stop her heart from galloping out of her chest.

'I haven't seen anything like it for about a year,' she agreed. 'Not at this time of year, anyway.'

'I enjoyed working with you again this morning,' he said unexpectedly, and there was no way she could keep her cheeks from heating up with the compliment. 'I confess that I was expecting things to be more awkward after the other night.'

'I was, too,' she admitted with a surprised laugh.

'You're a good doctor. Intuitive.'

Surely his approval shouldn't have made her fizz quite as much? Not that she was about to let him know. She lifted her shoulders in feigned casualness.

'And you're a good surgeon.'

They lapsed into silence for several long moments. He was close enough for her to smell him—a fresh, clean scent that reminded her of fine summer rain falling on the freshly mown fields in Meadwood—and close enough for her to feel the heat of his body, seeping through her scrubs and into her.

'Listen, can we sit for a moment and just clear the air after...the other night?'

There was no accusation in his tone, only a quiet sincerity. Relief unexpectedly rushed through Nell. She'd thought avoiding any mention of what had happened or not happened between them would have been better. It hadn't occurred to her that it could actually make things more awkward.

Clearing the air sounded like a far more preferable solution.

'Sure.' Turning to lead the way across the atrium floor, she headed for an empty table at the unusually quiet coffee shop and sat down.

And it was strange, wasn't it, how both a chaos and a kind of stillness washed over her at the very same time? Even her very blood felt as though it had begun to effervesce thrillingly in her veins, every particle in her anatomy hurtling dizzyingly into the path of another—like nothing she'd ever, *ever,* experienced before.

'First of all, I should apologise for the other night.'

And still her heart raced.

Should apologise? Or *was* he apologising? Or was the difference only in her head? As though he was apologising because he felt he ought to, not because he regretted kissing her? And maybe it was semantics, but she couldn't seem to help it; there was no denying the chemistry between them.

Yet pursuing anything beyond a professional relationship with Connor would surely only lead to trouble.

'I understand that things might initially be a bit awkward between us,' Connor said, breaking the silence. 'But if nothing else then today proved we work together well—professionally speaking.'

'We do,' she concurred.

Working with him to help their patient, James, had felt seamless—as it had with the patients they'd worked on before that...*interlude* between them back at her cottage. If she could just keep her thoughts in the professional arena rather than straying as they seemed to have a tendency to do these days. Namely, right back to the way his hands had felt on her skin, back to that vaguely spicy taste of his lips, back to the wantonness of her soft body pressed against the sheer male hardness of his.

Her entire body was already heating up at the memory. With an outstanding effort, Nell snapped her attention back to Connor.

'Why don't we put what happened the other night down to a momentary lapse in judgement? I value you as a colleague and I usually make it my business not to blur those lines. I suspect you do the same.'

She tried not to wrinkle her nose. He was entirely correct in his assessment of her—she'd only ever dated Jonathon, she'd never worked alongside him—and she supposed she should have been gratified in Connor's opinion of her. But somehow it only made her feel all the more frustrated.

'I do,' she said instead, though she wasn't certain she'd succeeded in keeping her voice completely steady.

Then again, his words seemed so careful. So formulaic. Was it possible that he was struggling as much as she was with the idea that there was still something...*unfinished* between them? Or was she imagining that, too?

'So, that's agreed, then?' His eyes held hers intently. 'We'll keep things exclusively professional from now on? Patients, and the hospital.'

'Of course.'

It was definitely for the best. Colleagues, and nothing more. If only she didn't fear it might require more willpower than she had. But if there was a voice in him that whispered about maybe wanting more—just as it needled in her—then he gave no indication.

'Right.' He inclined his head but made no move to stand up.

Neither, Nell noted, did she.

'And Vivian,' she heard herself add.

His forehead furrowed. Those two tiny lines right in the centre of his eyebrows that made her palms itch with the urge to trace them.

'Sorry?'

'Keeping things professional,' she reminded him. 'Patients, the hospital, and Vivian.'

He blinked. Slowly. Uncharacteristically.

'And Vivian,' he conceded after a moment. 'Yes, we need to work together for her, too.'

And that tension between them felt ramped as high as ever. Especially when neither of them seemed able to bring themselves to move even a muscle. Should she say something? Excuse herself back to work?

'I had intended to visit her after work.' Connor spoke just as she had willed herself to stand up. 'Or will you be going?'

She shook her head.

'I have to sort out the stall for the village's summer fete. Little Meadwood's Big Fete.'

'Ah, yes. Vintage clothing, wasn't it?'

'Right.' She was surprised he remembered.

'How is it going?'

'Well, I think I have most of the clothing together, though I ended up going in a bit of a steampunk direction in the end, but it's the actual build of stall that is proving a sticking point. I never was much of a DIY-er.'

'Would you like me to take a look?'

'You?' Her voice came out slightly higher pitched than she'd intended—hardly a surprise given that he was the last person she had expected to offer to help. Hastily, she sought to cover it up. 'What about keeping professional boundaries?'

'This is for Vivian.' He didn't shrug precisely, but there was some approximation of it. 'If she wants you to have a stall, then I can build it for you.'

'Right. Great. Still… I didn't know you were a builder.'

'I've been known to be handy with a drill or a saw. I've built cabinets, bookcases, and even constructed a new oak staircase once.'

She had to admit, the idea of having Connor's help appealed—though only for the *build* side of things, of course. Not because any part of her was that desperate to spend time with him.

'Are you trying to get brownie points from Vivian?' She sidestepped that line of thought immediately.

But there was no avoiding that delicious ripple that coursed through her when the corners of Connor's mouth turned up wryly.

'Naturally.'

Nell chuckled, shaking her head, glad that he retained his sense of humour despite the earlier awkwardness between them.

'Well, I certainly won't complain about the extra help.'

'Good.' Connor stood up, stunning her with a smile that was so different from the intensity of moments earlier. As if that had been the restrained Connor and this was now the real one. 'We'll make it the best stall at the fair.'

His grin was so infectious that Nell found herself smiling in response.

'Competitive much?'

'I make no apologies for it.' He laughed. The sound echoing thrillingly inside her as if mocking her earlier claims of just being friends. 'So, we'll start this weekend? Unless you're on duty.'

'I'm not,' she confirmed, urgently trying to slow her racing heart.

'Then this weekend it is.'

Before she could respond, he was walking away. Heading out of the opposite side of the atrium to where she needed to be, and yet the connection between them might as well have been a neon cord tying them together.

She really did need to get a grip. She couldn't help but be drawn to his confidence and competence, and, despite her earlier promise to herself, there was no ignoring the embers of attraction that still smouldered and crackled between them.

And unless she took major steps to control it, *that*, Nell decided firmly, threatened to derail the *professional relationship* they'd just agreed was paramount.

CHAPTER EIGHT

NELL WAS JUGGLING with the steampunk outfits, brass goggles and leather corsets that had spilled out of the stuffed bags and boxes and all over the boot of her car when she heard Connor's motorbike roaring down the lane towards her.

A tingle shot instantly down her spine. Not even a minute in and she was already failing at the 'keeping things strictly professional' part of the deal.

Great start, Nell.

Keeping her eyes focused on the goods, she set about shoving another purple corset and lace-up boot back into a bag as she pretended not to notice Connor pull up a few parking bays away and swing one motorbike-suited, muscular leg over his machine. Did he really have to be so attractive?

'Morning,' he called cheerily as he removed his sleek, aerodynamic crash helmet. 'Good day for it.'

'Great day,' she agreed, forcing a bright smile of her own. 'Forecast says it's going to be warm but not too hot, which is great if we're going to be working.'

'I heard. I even made a batch of Vivian's old summer mocktail recipe.'

'Really?' She straightened up as he headed over. 'That's amazing. So what's in the bag?'

'You said the theme was steampunk?' he checked, nodding as she waved her hand to the outfits in her car. 'Great, so I brought mechanical parts, cogs, tarnishing spray, all kinds of goodies.'

Nell peered into the bag he was opening up, caught off guard.

'That's a great idea. We can fix it around as decor.'

'Right.' Connor nodded. 'And I also thought the customers will need privacy to change into their steampunk costumes, so I could make some Shoji-like screens and tie them into the theme with cogs on the front.'

It took Nell a moment to regroup.

'That,' she told him sincerely, 'is a brilliant idea.'

'Seems like this is a bigger village fete than I ever remember it being,' Connor noted, heaving the bag onto his broad shoulders before leaning down to help her stuff the rest of the gear back into the boxes in her boot. 'I seem to remember it being quite a small community event.'

'It was,' she said with a sniff. 'It used to be quite a small, intimate affair, the kind where everyone knew everyone else. But with the new housing estates and the influx of new people to the area, it has become gradually bigger and flashier. In some ways that's good because it brings much-needed money into the village, but in another way it makes it more stressful because it's still up to the village committee to organise these events that now have to cater to hundreds. Even a thousand.'

'Looks like we have our work cut out for us, then.' Connor dipped his head, giving the impression that he wasn't the least bit fazed.

He probably wasn't. This was a man who looked as though he could handle anything.

Even, it seemed, being back in Little Meadwood after so many years of keeping his distance.

As they headed over to the old pavilion where the old stalls and timber were kept, Nell couldn't help but sneak glances at Connor out of the corner of her eye. He was carrying her boxes with complete ease, the muscles in his arms rippling as he expertly shifted them around. With his black leather motorcycle gear and aviator shades, he looked as though he had stepped straight out of being the stuntman for some action movie.

Of course he did.

Clucking her tongue in self-reproach, she tried to keep her mind on the task at hand. They needed to pick their stall, get it set up to see what needed repairing or replacing, and then start to add their decorations in a way that would make it bespoke for their theme. And woe betide them if they let Vivian down. It didn't help that there was already a considerable amount of activity by the pavilion; other villagers who clearly had the same idea to try to bag the better stall for themselves and avoid having to do complicated, time-consuming repairs.

'Plenty of people here.' He gritted his teeth, and

she couldn't help but notice how Connor's eyes were roaming everywhere.

Was this just his natural tendency to observe his surroundings or something more deliberate? An overhang from his military days, possibly.

'Do you want to leave? You don't have to help me, you know.'

And whatever had been bugging Connor, he seemed to regroup quickly.

'It isn't a problem,' he answered smoothly, setting down their gear on a good, flat area of land. 'Let's get to work.'

'Okay, then.' And just like that Nell felt a shiver of excitement at the prospect of tackling this challenge together.

Quickly and efficiently, Connor began to delve through the remaining stalls to decide which one was in the best shape before setting out his toolkit to begin assembling the structure. Nell, meanwhile, felt completely on the back foot as she fumbled with various pieces of wood and struggled to get anything to stay in place.

'Here, let me help,' Connor said, coming over to her and grasping her hand. A jolt of electricity shot up her arm at the contact, though she instructed herself to ignore it as he led her through the steps of assembling the stall. They worked in silence for a while, each lost in their own thoughts, until Connor spoke up.

'You know, Nell, I never would have taken you

for a steampunk aficionado,' he said, glancing over at her.

She looked up at him, surprised. 'What do you mean?'

'I don't know, I guess I just never would have imagined you being into something so…alternative,' he said with a grin.

Nell feigned an indignant laugh. 'What's wrong with being different?'

'Not one thing,' he replied, returning to his task, though she hadn't missed the teasing glint in his eyes. 'Truth be told, I think it's hot.'

Heat suffused her cheeks at the compliment and she couldn't stop herself from stealing another glance at him before turning away to busy herself rearranging the tools.

'The rest of these screwheads are too chewed up to use.' He sighed. 'I think I might need to invest in some supplies. Is Jay's hardware shop still around?'

Nell shook her head sadly.

'No, he died and his son sold up and moved away. However, there's a big chain in the city who usually send us stuff each year. I think you'll find boxes of screws and nails, and maybe hinges, on the metal racks at the back of the pavilion. Plus, there are recycling bins for junk. Metal in one for scrapyard sales, and another one for wood that could go towards the Bonfire Night celebrations.'

'Wow, it's all go here at Little Meadwood, isn't it?'

'We've tried to move with the times,' she agreed,

grateful they were back to less awkward conversation. The longer they worked together, the more she realised that Connor's easy banter and infectious laugh were the perfect antidote to the stress of building their stall. It should definitely make it easier to work around the hospital with him, without her mind constantly creeping back to that night together.

Nell felt a flutter in her stomach at his smile. She quickly shook her head, trying to push the thought away. She was here to work, not to get involved with Connor. But when his hand brushed against hers as they both reached for the same screwdriver, she couldn't help but feel that familiar spark of electricity between them. Especially when the summer day began to heat up and Connor stripped down to a simple black sleeveless tee, his lean muscles rippling in a way that made it almost impossible for her to concentrate on her own tasks.

All he needed was a can of pop, a rock-song soundtrack, and he could have been the next hot advert.

She shook her head as if to dislodge the X-rated image and forced herself to focus on her job. Easier said than done.

Bit by bit, they organised their stall, unloaded more from the boxes and bags in her car. With Connor's expertise and Nell's eye for detail, they soon had the steampunk-themed decor up and running like clockwork. They even managed to add a touch of Victorian class with an antique mirror and a few brass lamps. It was perfect.

Finally they stepped back to admire their handiwork.

'It looks amazing,' she breathed proudly.

'It does,' he agreed, lifting one dusty forearm to wipe a bead of sweat from above his eyebrow. 'I have to say that I think we make a pretty good team.'

Nell laughed. 'Not that I'm surprised, but I do have to admit it's been fun working with you. It's been a while since I've had such a good laugh.'

'Well, I'm glad to be here to remind you to have some fun.'

'And I'm glad to be reminded that you're more than capable of handling anything thrown your way,' she added, shooting him a sly smile.

Connor's eyes shone with amusement. 'I have my moments.'

Nell rolled her eyes. 'You're too modest. You're probably one of the most capable people I know.'

'Flattery will get you everywhere,' he replied with a chuckle.

Nell laughed and nudged his shoulder playfully. 'Don't get too full of yourself now.'

They stood there for a moment longer, admiring their handiwork, before Nell sighed and turned to him. 'Well, I guess that's it. We're all set up.'

'Looks like it, yeah,' he agreed, glancing around

at the other stalls that were still being assembled. 'Photo for Vivian.'

'That's a great idea.'

Scurrying over to her bag, she retrieved her phone and then they both positioned themselves in front of the stall. She wasn't prepared for him to lean in closer to her and wrap his arm around her waist—hopefully he wouldn't notice that she slowed down a little to take the photo, indulging in the unexpected moment.

Was it just her imagination that he also seemed to linger a little?

'I should probably get going,' she told him reluctantly when they finally moved back apart. 'I have a list of things to pick up from the shop, and I don't want to keep her waiting.'

Connor nodded. 'I'll help you pack up and get everything to your car.'

Nell nodded uncertainly and they set to work, carefully dismantling the stall and setting it in a bay where she chalked their names on the board. Any loose decor was packed back into the boxes and stacked in the same bay to make it easier on the set-up weekend. And then all that was left was to load the remaining supplies into Nell's car and say their goodbyes. But instead of each of them returning to their vehicles, she hovered by the open door of her car as he leaned his bottom on her bonnet, his impossibly long legs stretched out in front of him.

'Well, thanks for a more entertaining day than I was expecting.'

'You're...welcome?' she hazarded with another laugh and tipped her face upwards.

Despite the warmth of the summer sun on her face all she could feel was the cold regret that the day was over. Being with Connor had been fun: natural and effortless. She didn't want it to end.

He shifted on the bonnet, his eyes meeting hers, and she felt the energy between them once again.

'Seriously though, Nell, I had a really great time.'

'Me too,' she replied softly, her heart thudding in her chest. 'I'm almost sorry it's over.'

He offered a lopsided grin. 'Who says it has to be over?'

Nell's eyes widened in surprise, and she stared at him in confusion. 'What do you mean?'

Connor shrugged.

'Maybe we should end the successful day with a drink? Celebrate a job well done?'

Nell hesitated, the logical part of her brain telling her that this was a bad idea. But the rest of her was screaming *yes*. She hadn't been on a date in months, hadn't felt this kind of attraction to someone in even longer. And she was tired of letting her fears hold her back.

'Okay,' she said finally, trying to keep her voice calm and steady. 'I'd like that.'

Connor's smile widened, and he hopped off the

bonnet, coming closer to her. 'Great. I'll see you later?'

Nell nodded, her heart beating faster with each passing moment. 'Sounds good but where? The Willow Tree pub?'

'No. Nothing local. How about heading back to town? There's a bar by the river I've heard is good.'

'Okay.' She glanced over at his bike, then down at her clothes. 'I need a shower and change first. Should I meet you there?'

He flashed a smile.

'I wouldn't mind a shower, either. How about I pick you up in a couple of hours?'

'On your motorbike?' She looked dubious.

'It's a great bike.' Connor laughed. 'Plus, I have a spare crash helmet.'

Was he joking?

'I don't know what I'm supposed to wear to ride a motorbike,' she hedged. 'I guess I can just leave my hair in a ponytail?'

A grin tugged at his lips.

'Relax. I'm only teasing. Wear whatever you want. I'll ditch the bike back at the hospital and I'll pick you up in a taxi.'

'Oh, I should just meet you there. You don't have to go to that much trouble.'

'I want to.'

She tried not to look too thrilled. He'd clearly thought this through—it wasn't just an offhand invitation.

'Okay. Great.'

As Connor crossed over to his motorbike to head back to the city to clean up, Nell leaned against the door frame of her car, feeling the cool metal press against her overheated skin. The idea of having a drink with Connor felt ridiculously exciting. More than exciting, actually. It felt like something she had been missing out on for a long time.

How was it that she felt so changed from herself every time Connor Mason was near? As if she were caught up in a thrilling whirlwind every time he was in the vicinity.

As if he *were* the whirlwind.

And maybe that was what she needed right now—as long as she remembered not to get too deeply involved. It was just fun. After all, she was rooted in Little Meadwood; it was where her foster family were, where her friends were, where her career was. Connor, on the other hand, was just passing through. A proverbial rolling stone on the lookout for his next adventure. The very opposite of her.

Which, she conceded, might have been one of the reasons she felt so drawn to this transient soul. Connor's free spirit seemed to have ignited a restless fire in her that she hadn't ever realised was there before. A reminder that life was meant to be lived. And it had made her begin to question whether Jonathon might have been right all along when he'd accused her of hiding out in Little Meadwood.

She'd sunk into its relative safety the day she'd

been brought here after her parents' deaths. It had been both her comfort and her safety net, and Vivian had always been there to catch her if she fell.

But now, as Nell stood there, contemplating the possibilities of a night out with Connor, she couldn't help but wonder if it was time to let go of that safety net and take a leap of faith.

Even if just this once.

'I've never been here before,' Nell admitted as they walked down the quayside where the taxi had dropped them off, to the trendy bar he'd chosen.

'Neither have I.' He grinned. 'I've just seen it a few times when out running in the evening, thought it looked good and heard a couple of positive reviews. The view is definitely worth seeing.'

'It is,' she agreed, standing with him for a moment to appreciate the lights shimmering across the water.

With only the low bass line of faraway music floating on the air, it was a peaceful and calming summer evening.

Or at least, it should have been peaceful and calming, if only Nell didn't faze him in that intrinsic way of hers. He didn't want to notice it, certainly not allow himself to get caught up by it. Yet nor could he seem to ignore it, and pretend it wasn't there, this pull that he felt towards her.

And right now, those stunning morpho-blue pools of hers sparkled in the marine light, holding an expression that he didn't care to examine but that made his chest ache all the same.

They moved off again, walked in silence towards the bar and Connor couldn't help but feel as if he was walking into dangerous territory. No matter how much he reminded himself that pursuing anything with Nell was a bad idea, he couldn't keep his eyes off her. Not least the way her dress hugged her curves in all the right places as she weaved her way through the crowd.

He would far, far rather have been somewhere else with her. Somewhere they could be alone. Private.

God, he was in trouble.

The bar was larger than he'd expected, the sounds of laughter and music filling the air as they boarded. Couples and groups of friends were scattered across the floor, drinks in hand, dancing to the beat of the music. And then Nell seemed to recognise one group, greeting them with a smile and a hug. Connor watched her, fascinated by the way she moved so gracefully and effortlessly—so unlike the guarded way he was around strangers. She was a breath of fresh air. Her laugh was infectious, her conversation was witty and intelligent, and her touch sent the most delicious shivers coursing through him. He couldn't remember the last time he had felt such a strong connection with someone, and it scared him.

Or it ought to have done.

But before he could consider that further someone

jostled against Nell, propelling her forwards into his arms. And he ought to be more concerned that the urge to kiss her was almost dangerously overwhelming. One tiny tilt of his head and he could capture her mouth all too easily, tasting those deliciously plump lips that were too perfectly pink for their own good.

But he couldn't. He mustn't. It was too risky, too dangerous, and everything that he'd warned himself about.

And yet he was the one who had invited her out for a drink.

Still, their bodies shifted and swayed together—the perfect fit. And before he realised it, they were dancing right there on the floor amongst the other couples, whilst this fire inside him burned hotter, brighter, consuming him as it made it impossible for him to think of anything else.

'Are you okay?' Nell murmured, her warm breath teasing his neck as though she sensed his inner turmoil.

'Fine,' he managed, not trusting himself to say anything more than that.

He ought to stop this now. Step away from her.

Instead he stayed exactly where he was with his arms wrapped around her delectable body, and his mind pushing that warning voice further and further back until it was too muffled to hear. And perhaps they stayed like that for ten minutes, perhaps ten lifetimes.

Connor had no idea how he finally managed to break apart.

'So, what can I get you to drink?'

And what did it say that he enveloped her hand in his as they made their way to the bar, and neither of them made any attempt to let go, even when the crowd was so thick that they'd had to crush together? By the time they reached the bar, Nell's body was still pressed up against his and he was wholly caught up in the magic of it.

In a daze that he wanted never to end.

Before he could stop himself, Connor leaned in closer, his lips brushing against her ear, and when Nell pulled her head back to look up at him, her blue eyes so dark that he thought they might almost be black, his fragile resolve crumbled completely and he finally dipped his head to hers. Possibly the gentlest, most tender kiss he'd ever given any woman before—yet it held all the unspoken words between them. Nell's lips were so soft, so pliant as she kissed him back, so gloriously inviting that they made his heart race enough that he didn't think he could remember his own name.

Enough to make the rest of the bar—the rest of the world—disappear.

But then a loud cry abruptly shattered the peace. A woman's voice, high-pitched and panicked, screaming for a doctor.

Nell and Connor sprang apart abruptly, and Connor pushed through the already shifting crowd before exiting the bar and turning down the quayside in the direction of the cry. Instinct told him that Nell wasn't far behind. Sprinting together, they soon reached a small crowd gathering around and on the steps of a small houseboat and pushed their way through the gathering people until they finally saw her—a woman in her late fifties, perhaps, with a bloodied sundress and an ashen face, kneeling over a boy, maybe ten years old, who was lying motionless on the deck of the boat.

'Let us through, please,' Connor commanded, leading the way as he clambered aboard with Nell. 'We're doctors.'

'Are you the mother?' he ascertained even as he raced to the child to begin his initial assessment.

Behind him, Nell was lifting her voice to address the crowd.

'Has someone called for an ambulance? Okay, you, sir, with that phone…yes, you. Call emergency services and tell them that we have an unconscious child, and give them the location to get an ambulance en route. Then stay on the line to them and wait for us to feed you more information. Got it? Great.'

Dimly, Connor heard Nell's commands but he had concerns of his own. It was clear the boy had been stabbed—by the looks of it with a long, wide blade. Connor grabbed a nearby tea towel to staunch the bleeding even as his eyes darted around for a weapon. The last thing he wanted to do was to put Nell in any danger.

'What happened here?' he demanded sharply to the mother.

Connor was aware of Nell dealing with the growing crowd of onlookers.

'My h-h-husband was just making us a drink,' the woman hiccupped. 'I w-wanted lemon so he went to cut one. He was carrying the knife. He… fell down those steps just as…just as our son came out of his bedroom.'

Connor glanced around again. A couple of lemons were lodged against the baseboards of the kitchen area, as well as a long knife. The half-prepped drinks were still on the counter, and a cuddly toy was lying, dropped, by the dining table.

'Where's your husband now?'

'I…don't know…' The woman looked stunned. Clearly her priority had been her son. 'He fell.'

'He's here,' Nell exclaimed, hurrying across the deck to the floor on the other side of the counter, out of Connor's line of sight. 'Unconscious, with an open head injury.'

'Update the operator,' Connor instructed the man with the phone, watching as Nell began her ABCs.

'Did he fall, or did he trip, then fall?' Connor asked quickly.

If the man tripped, that was one thing. But if he tripped then fell, there could be an underlying issue. Heart attack, stroke—the list was long.

'He…tripped.'

The woman was beginning to cry again, and Connor took care to keep his voice calm and kind, but firm.

'Do you have a first-aid kit?'

The woman gave a jerky nod.

'Good. You need to get your first-aid kit. And some towels. Hurry.'

'Ambulance is on its way,' the man in the crowd called out.

'Make sure they send two.' Connor lifted his head as the man nodded in acknowledgement.

'Airway, breathing, circulation all okay here,' Nell called as quietly as she could. 'Looks like he slammed his head on the corner of the unit as he fell. I think he's starting to come around, but as soon as the wife comes back I'll get her to keep his head and shoulders slightly elevated.'

'The boy has just stopped breathing,' Connor muttered in a low voice, turning his attention back to their unexpected patient. 'We need to perform CPR.'

Nodding wordlessly, Nell carefully moved her patient into a safe position before hurrying across the floor to sit herself by the boy's head whilst Connor began chest compressions. He was counting under his breath as he went and she counted with him, thirty compressions followed by two rescue breaths.

Then again.

And again.

And again.

But the CPR wasn't working.

'First-aid kit.' The woman reappeared, thrusting it to them with shaking hands. 'It's a good one. My husband always insisted on good first-aid kits.'

'First ambulance is twenty minutes out,' the phone man called out at that moment.

'You need to do something.' Connor sensed, rather than saw, Nell's gaze on him. 'The kid doesn't have twenty minutes.'

He had already come to the same conclusion. There was only one option left to him.

'Get everyone out of here,' he murmured to Nell. 'Including the mother.'

Nell offered a silent nod. They both knew that cutting through the sternum would make a noise that no parent should ever have to hear. Though he suspected little could be worse than the absolute silence on the boat at this moment.

Connor worked quickly and methodically, prepping the boy for the emergency surgery and sterilising his hands, and whatever tools he could find to perform the operation. At least the kit contained a few pairs of surgical gloves. Behind him, he heard Nell command everyone off the vessel, returning sooner than he'd expected with two more strangers in tow.

'We've got two nurses from City,' Nell explained quickly. 'They were in a nearby restaurant when they heard the shouts.'

'Great,' Connor acknowledged with a quick nod. 'Thanks for heading over. Could one of you take over care of the male and the other keep the mother out of the way? Nell, you're here with me.'

Having both his and Nell's full attention on the boy was a much better scenario, and as the two nurses efficiently took up their roles he felt more comfortable focusing on his own patient.

'Okay, here we go.'

Working quickly and methodically, Connor began to cut open the boy's chest with Nell instinctively moving to help, holding the lungs clear as he took care to avoid the phrenic and intercostal nerves.

'Just move your left hand here,' he indicated after a moment. 'I can't afford to risk any injury to the pulmonary vessels right there. Yes, good.'

They worked seamlessly together until the young boy's heart was finally exposed and Connor could begin compressions directly onto the organ.

One...

Two...

Three...

Four...

Five...

And the boy was back with them, that welcome sight of the young heart pulsing back into life. Relief coursed through him, and from the emotion in Nell's expressive blue eyes when they snagged his, she was feeling just as charged.

'The paramedics are here.' One of the nurses suddenly appeared by their sides, and he realised that several more people were now on the deck, standing out of the way but ready to step in whenever he gave them the all-clear. 'The father has already gone with the first crew.'

'Right.' Connor nodded, his eyes not leaving his patient.

'They're going to need you to be with the boy in the ambulance,' Nell muttered in a low voice.

'Of course,' Connor agreed. 'But it won't be an easy journey either way. Okay, just put your hands exactly where mine are now. No, a little more…yes. There. Hold steady like that.'

He didn't need to voice the words to tell her that the chances of the boy surviving the ambulance ride to the hospital weren't all that good.

CHAPTER NINE

'I HOPE HE makes it.' Nell heaved a deep breath as she and Connor headed out of the hospital doors half an hour later. The paramedic driving had manoeuvred the ambulance through the mercifully quiet roads like some world-class driver, and they had miraculously got the boy to the hospital without further incident. The on-call trauma surgeon had swept the boy straight into surgery, and he was being operated on even at that moment.

'Time will tell,' Connor replied carefully.

His standard response, but she knew that in surgery it was often the only real truth. Her mind searched for something else to add, and it took her a moment to realise that Connor had stopped walking.

'I should have thought to book a taxi back to Little Meadwood whilst we were inside.'

'Good point.'

It hadn't even crossed her mind. The truth was she didn't even want to go. Too much energy ran through her veins; she was far too agitated and fidgety.

At least that was what she told herself.

'I'll go back in and call.'

It shouldn't have taken her so much effort to force her legs into action to walk away.

'Wait.' She'd stopped even before he'd finished the command. 'There's blood on your dress. And your jacket thing.'

'It's a bolero,' she answered as her hand flew instinctively to the fabric—more for something to say than anything else.

She glanced down at herself in dismay. She was very aware of what she had been through just moments before and, looking down, there was a stark reminder of it on her clothes.

'Ah, a taxi driver might not be too happy about me getting in like this.'

'Do you have spare clothes in your locker?'

'Usually.' Her smile was rueful. 'But I took them home yesterday to freshen them all up. I figured I'd take them back when I'm on shift on Monday.'

Connor didn't answer at first, his eyes scanning around them as if he was deciding on the best solution.

'You could come back to mine,' he offered at length, indicating the accommodation block just across the park. 'We can get the worst of the stain out and call a taxi.'

'That would be great.' She flashed him a bright smile, as though she were oblivious to the flutter of nerves in her stomach.

The night had been unexpectedly chaotic, but now she was coming down from the adrenalin of it, Nell found her thoughts were winding their way back to the kiss she and Connor had shared moments before they'd heard that first scream. As they began to walk through the prettily lit park, her heart was thumping harder and harder as if in anticipation.

Life was so damned short. Hadn't tonight been a stark reminder of that?

Nell couldn't keep denying the attraction between the two of them. More to the point, she didn't want to.

And then, they were there. And Connor was unlocking the door of his apartment and standing back to allow her to go in first.

The suite was like nothing she'd imagined. Surgeons' quarters or not, it was certainly unlike any of the hospital accommodation she'd stayed in during her training.

'This place is stunning,' she exclaimed.

Sharp, clean lines ran through the walls, ceilings, all converging on a large picture window that framed the park through which they'd just walked, with the hospital lights twinkling beyond. Like one of the most artistic urban pictures. Clearly not all the apartments would be like this one—this one was reserved for surgeons like Connor—but even so, the building was impressive.

'You've never been in here before?' Connor frowned.

'No. I saw it being built, of course, and I saw the architectural drawings.'

'Understood.' He nodded, striding through to the

kitchen and reaching to a sleek, push-to-open cupboard. 'I'll get something to clean up those stains.'

A moment later he turned back carrying a damp cloth and a bottle of stain remover.

'You deal with your dress, and I'll take care of your...what did you call it...bolero thing?'

She nodded mutely, shrugging it off and handing it to him as surprise coursed through her. But even as she began dealing with the bloodstains on her dress it was impossible to stop her eyes from sliding to Connor as he worked. The muscles that rippled beneath his shirt made her cheeks flush with heat, reminding her of the sight of his bare chest that night in her cottage.

As if sensing her gaze, he lifted his head and, to her chagrin, caught her staring.

Too late, she snatched her gaze away, the heat in her cheeks growing hotter by the second.

'Sorry,' she mumbled, not even certain what she was apologising for.

She certainly wasn't prepared when he reached out and took her chin in his hand, turning her face back towards him.

'Don't be,' he said, his voice low, urgent. 'I like it when you look at me like that.'

And then, before she could register what was happening, Connor leaned in and kissed her. Warm, soft lips that sent jolts of electricity shooting through her body. For a moment, she was lost in the sensation, forgetting everything else.

But then, just as suddenly, he pulled back.

'I shouldn't have done that,' he said, his eyes troubled. 'I'm sorry.'

Nell felt a pang of disappointment.

'No,' she murmured firmly. 'Not again.'

'Not again, what?'

'You can't keep starting and stopping something over and over again,' she told him urgently. 'It's like a gravity ride, throwing me around everywhere until I'm dizzy and disorientated, not knowing which way is even up.'

'So, you wanted me to stop?' he gritted out, as if fighting himself more than her.

Sensations jostled in her chest.

'No,' she whispered. 'I want to know you *won't* stop. Not this time.'

Connor lifted his hand to her face, his thumb gently brushing over her cheekbone, his eyes practically black with desire.

'You're sure?'

'I'm sure.'

She'd barely even finished before he was lowering his head, his mouth claiming hers. Fierce, fiery, and full of passion. And all she could do was melt against the solid wall of his chest, melding her body to his, feeling herself grow weak yet powerful all at the same time. His mouth moved over hers, his tongue sliding expertly over her lips, teasing and coaxing as she parted them to let him inside. She clung to him, her fingers biting into the muscular lines of his shoulders as though if she let go, she might tumble into the fire within, even as she felt the flames lick at her and begin to consume her from the inside out.

Slowly, painstakingly, his hands started their exploration of her body, as if they had all the time in the world and he intended to use every millisecond of it getting every single inch of her in the most intimate detail. It was so gloriously indulgent that at one point she thought she forgot even to breathe. Connor's fingers trailed over her skin like a thousand tiny sparks sprinkled liberally over every line, every curve of her flesh. She found herself arching into his touch, an almost feverish anticipation making her body tremble. He traced whorls over her back, brushed patterns down each of her sides in turn, and slid his fingertips over the dip of her throat where his thumbpad made long, slow circles, making her feel like some exotic flower blooming for the first time in a century.

And when he buried his head to lay a wreath of kisses down the column of her neck from her ear to her shoulder, each one made her quiver that little bit more, sending her further and further to places she'd never been before.

Not like this.

There was something about him that was deeply intense, and he seemed to be leaving his mark upon her. Her thoughts, that the last thing she needed was another roller-coaster romance, seemed to be at odds with the way she felt.

But this connection between them was powerful and fierce, and it was impossible to deny it.

Nell wound her arms around his neck, pulling him closer. No matter how long they touched, tasted, explored, it didn't seem to be enough. The yawning ache in her just kept growing, wanting more. And more again. He was like a summer storm—thunder and lightning, rain and wind, all hurtling together, crashing and exploding around them until they found themselves in the very centre…in that perfect calmness as he lifted his mouth from hers, breaking contact.

Then he rested his forehead against hers, his eyes like bottomless depths, in which she could almost imagine she saw a future.

She shoved the errant thought away and struggled to catch a breath.

'Stay here tonight,' he managed, his voice raw.

'I thought you'd never ask,' she replied with a shaky laugh.

The primal growl in his throat seemed to pool right *there*…at the apex of her legs.

In one smooth motion he was scooping her up into his arms and carrying her through to his bedroom. The soft light filtering through the windows casting flickering shadows and leaving a warm glow over the room. Gently, he laid her on the bed before standing over her. Taking her in as if she were his own personal gift that he was admiring before he even began to start opening it.

But the waiting was killing her, and before Nell could register what she was doing, she had lifted her hands to wind them around Connor's neck and draw him down on top of her.

'I'm sure I warned you not to stop,' she managed to tease, before pulling his lower lip into her mouth with just the right amount of tenderness and demand that made him groan in response.

As if he was nowhere near as in control as she'd thought he was. The knowledge gave her an unexpected boost.

'Take this off,' she managed huskily against his mouth, her fingers toying with the hem of his black tee.

'Now you're giving orders?' he rasped.

It took all she had to respond.

'I'm trying. You're not obeying.'

The look he shot her was practically searing. Making her feel white-hot inside before shattering her. If this was all they would ever have together, then it would be a night she could cherish for ever.

'I approve of this side of you.' His tone was guttural.

'Still not obeying.'

He drew back from her at last, and she felt the loss acutely. But then his gaze snared hers, long and hard, as his eyes narrowed over her. That wickedly sensuous mouth of his far too far away from her pleasure.

'Then consider me yours to command,' he bit out after what felt like an age. 'For now.'

Was he really serious? Lying there, his body covering hers, he was really going to let her call the shots?

'Strip off,' she instructed, barely recognising her own voice.

She hadn't been entirely convinced he would simply comply, but Nell found herself propping herself up on her elbows in disbelief as he slid his body off hers, hard masculine lines grating deliciously over her as he stood up at the end of the bed and did precisely that. First hooking his tee over his head to reveal the most sinful set of abs that Nell had spent the past few weeks thinking she must have surely imagined being so damned perfect.

And then he moved his hand to his belt, unbuckling it with such a tantalising sound that it defied belief. Her mouth felt parched as he hooked his thumbs over the waistband and pushed his trousers and boxers down, discarding them to the side. Standing there, naked and unabashed in front of her—not that anything about Connor Mason had ever seemed the slightest bit *abashed*. His desire for her on show for them both to see.

'Satisfied?' he demanded, amusement unmistakable in his voice.

She swallowed once. Twice. Flicking her tongue out of her suddenly dry lips.

'I hope so,' she just about managed.

As if an aching heat weren't pooling between her legs where she needed him most.

'And what about you?' Connor drawled. 'Are you going to remain so…overdressed?'

It took her several moments to realise that it was she who was breathing so heavily.

'I think I'll leave that to you,' she uttered at last.

And it was apparently all the encouragement Connor needed. Smoothly drawing her dress up her legs, he reached around to cup each of her thighs in each of his hands, before sliding down the bed towards her. Then, without the slightest preamble, he sank to the floor, hooked aside the scrap of lace that barely even pretended to cover her modesty, and sank his face between her legs.

Fireworks went off all around Nell in an instant.

Nothing, *no one*, had ever made her feel so sexy. So wanton. So wanted.

He licked her, teased her, and ran those long, lean fingers of his up her inner thighs and round to hold her backside, lifting her closer up towards him as if to give himself better access. Her hips could do nothing but undulate appreciatively under his control, bucking and writhing as if they had a life of their own. No restraints, no inhibitions, she was all his—and he knew it. Over and over, he brought her to the edge, then made her back off. He trailed kisses up one leg then down the other, lazy licks wreaking havoc on her senses, until he flicked one devastatingly skilled tongue where she needed him most. Sensations unlike any she'd experienced before skittered up and down and all around her, pleasure warring with an almost unbearable ache for more.

So much more.

Raw need scraped at her as she speared her hands through his hair. And finally, when she didn't think she could take it any longer, he slid his finger inside her, his mouth still licking, and tasting and toying. The waves began to build higher than ever; Connor stoking them with every sublime sweep of his roguish tongue.

And then, finally, with one skilful twist of his wrist, Nell felt her muscles tighten around him and her nails dig into the skin of his back as he tossed her over the edge and into the fires below. Hot, intense, and all-consuming.

All she could hope was that he'd be there to pull her out of them before they incinerated her completely.

Connor felt the shudder of Nell's orgasm ripple through her entire body, and a possessive heat raced through his veins.

All mine.

He pulled back to gaze into her face, watching her eyes slowly flutter open as the pleasure subsided. Slowly. Perfectly.

Her cheeks were flushed, her lips soft and parted, and the look of sheer bliss on her face made his chest swell. Something so primitive coursed through his veins, making his pulse race so hard that he was shocked it didn't rock the entire room.

But he was just a man—and never a very good man, at that—and the longer he watched her, the more his body ached to be inside. To join with her on whatever journey she was on right now. To make her scream his name even louder than he suspected she hadn't realised she'd cried out just now. The need to bury himself inside her—inside this particular, maddening woman—was almost his undoing. As if there were some caged beast inside him, raging and roaring and fighting to break free.

He would never know how he managed to wait for her to come back to earth again.

'What…' she seemed to be having trouble articulating her thoughts '…was…that?'

'That,' he growled, taking in the way she was subconsciously arching her body towards him as if still subtly begging for more, 'was starters.'

'Starters?' she echoed, dazedly.

'Starters. But this is the main course.'

And then he dispensed with her dress and the rest of her ridiculously flimsy, lacy underwear with a haste that might have been unseemly had he even cared about such propriety. Then, his brain just about reminding him in time to slip on protection, he covered her now naked body with his own.

Flesh to flesh. Hot and flawless. Just like his Nell.

He kissed one breast, then the other, letting both

his fingers and his tongue explore the valley that parted them. And all the while, he used his tip to tease at her core. He dipped in, then out again, revelling in the way her hips rose with him in a silent plea for more. And he would never reveal to her just what it took not to plunge deeper, right there, right then.

But then, if he did that, how could he keep enjoying the motion, the pleasure, the connection?

The connection.

It felt like some kind of sacrament. Sacred and pure. Something that would only ever be meant for the two of them. The way their bodies melded as though they were tailor-made for each other.

He moved his hips, dipping in that little bit deeper before withdrawing again, taking them both higher. Faster. Indulging in the sheer pleasure of her slickness around him, and the way she gripped him, as if trying to stop him from leaving her.

'If this is the main course…' the words juddered out of Nell as she sighed '…then I don't think I'll ever look at another meal the same way again.'

'I'm counting on it,' he growled.

And then he thrust into her. Deep, and hard, and true. Rewarded when Nell threw her legs around his torso and locked her heels, her nails grazing his back as she held on. A thing of wondrous beauty that made him think that he could do anything…

If only this woman would be in his arms like this. Every night.

For ever.

But that made no sense. Connor pushed the thoughts aside as he threw himself fully into the moment. Moving faster, deeper, building that tempo as he grazed one hand over the soft swell of her silken abdomen, making her tremble with need.

There was nothing about her that didn't fascinate him. That didn't call to the basest parts of him. She was everything he'd never known he wanted. And more. She made his world tilt and spin, yet at the same time she somehow made it make more sense than it ever had in his life before. The way she made him feel so intoxicated, with lights and colours spilling out of her and breathing life into his whole world.

So, what was he supposed to do with that knowledge?

And then it didn't matter because she groaned his name and every last thought slid from his head as he gave himself up to the hold she had over him. Every touch, every kiss, every thrust, and he still couldn't get enough of her; of their synchronised rhythm, and the way her body was wracked with pulses of need that made him feel powerful and humble all at once.

Finally, *finally*, Connor gave in to every last wild pull, throwing them both off the edge and hoping that they'd never have to reach the bottom.

Or that, at least, they'd manage to find a safe landing once it was all over.

CHAPTER TEN

NELL WOKE SOMETIME in the early hours.

Beside her, the bed was cold. Empty. Yet the room didn't feel as though she was alone.

Sitting up straight, she peered into the darkness—allowing her eyes time to adjust. And then she saw him. Silhouetted against the window by the moon's soft glow, his back to the bed whilst his focus seemed trained outside, into the blackness of the space, as if that was where he wished he could go.

Far away from City Hospital. Even further away from Little Meadwood.

'Connor?' She spoke his name quietly. 'Are you okay?'

He startled fractionally, as if he hadn't realised she'd woken.

'Fine.' His voice was gritty. 'I didn't intend to wake you. Go back to sleep.'

'Come back to bed, then,' she urged gently.

She heard, rather than saw, him brace his hands on the window frame.

'I can't promise this...*thing* between us can lead to anything.'

'I know that.'

He said he couldn't promise…but did that mean he was considering it? Her heart leapt before she could rein it in.

'I can't even promise how long I can stay. Not indefinitely, anyway.'

'I didn't ask for more than that.' She tried to sound lighter, airier, than she felt, though she wasn't sure he even heard her. 'Why do you hate Little Meadwood so much?'

She wasn't sure she knew what had made her ask, but the question had just seemed to tumble out.

There was a beat before he answered.

'Who said I hate it?' His voice was even and controlled. Perhaps *too* controlled.

'So, I'm wrong?'

The silence swirled around them for a long moment. So long that Nell slid her legs slowly round and got out of bed, moving across the bedroom to stand behind him. She half expected him to move away but when he didn't, she summoned all her courage and rested her chin against Connor's back. As though she could somehow lend him support.

'Is it because Little Meadwood reminds you of your mother?'

'My mother?' He half turned, his voice sharp. Catching her off guard.

'You came to Vivian after your mother died, didn't you?' she pointed out carefully. 'When you were six?'

And she couldn't have explained what it was that

caused a shift in the silence so that it felt suddenly fraught. Loaded.

She shifted her weight from one foot to the other uncertainly, not really expecting him to answer.

'I do understand, you know. My parents' passing was how I came to have Vivian as a foster mother.'

'Except that you love Little Meadwood.' His voice was so low that she almost had to strain to hear. 'You've made a life there. To you, it's a bucolic place filled with happy memories.'

'I know you don't see it that way.'

'No, I do not,' he rasped. 'To me…it was a prison. One to which I swore I would never, *ever* return.'

He paused, as if choosing his words, but Nell simply waited. Giving him time.

'If it wasn't for Vivian—the one woman who has been probably the closest I've ever had to a maternal figure—I never would have come back.'

He shook his head. Hard. But she still didn't answer—she didn't want to risk interrupting him and causing him to clam up again.

'It's a small village where people are on top of each other, and everyone knows everyone else's business—moreover, everyone sticks their noses into everyone else's business.' Even in the low light she could see him twist his face up into an expression of disdain, his breath heaving as if he'd been out on one of his ten-mile runs. 'And the sins of a parent cling to a child, no matter how innocent that child might be. Or how innocent any child *ought to* be.'

Nell reached out as though to squeeze his shoulder but then decided better of it. She still didn't answer. The truth was that she didn't know what to say. Everybody knowing everybody else's business was one of the things she had always loved most about Little Meadwood. It had made her feel as though the place were just one big, close-knit family.

But she knew many of the other foster children hadn't shared her sentimentality.

'That place taught me the harsh lesson that when you're the dirty, half-feral kid of a single, junkie mother then, no matter what goes wrong in the village, you'll always be the first one to feel the jabbing fingers of blame. For nine years, from the age of six right up until that very last day, almost a decade later, I was the *outsider*. Never to be trusted.'

'Oh, Connor,' she whispered. This time her hand did manage to reach out to cup his upper arm.

As if that could somehow help.

'Someone left a gate open and Tom Rickman's prize bull escaped...?' he gritted out. 'Blame the Mason kid.'

She squeezed his arm but didn't speak.

'Someone stole a bunch of chocolate from the local corner shop?' he continued bitterly. 'That Mason boy was definitely spotted in the vicinity.'

'It wasn't always like that, was it?' she whispered, an incredible wave of sadness washing over her.

It had been so different for her.

'Always.' He snorted bitterly. 'Someone smoked a cigarette behind the cricket pavilion that doubled as a youth centre on the green and inadvertently set fire to the dried-out, rotten timber decking…?' This time, he pulled a grim face, despite himself. 'Well, okay, so that time I had actually been one of the lads stupid enough to be smoking there. But it hadn't been my discarded cigarette end.'

'I'm so sorry,' she managed at last, her voice thick with emotion.

She wasn't even sure if Connor heard her.

'But recently, I've been wondering what came first.' His voice was little more than a rasp. 'The village folk being right about me being rebellious, and *trouble* even as a six-year-old? Or the idea that they were going to blame me whether I was guilty or not, so I might as well be hung for a sheep as a lamb, as that old proverb goes?'

Nell wasn't sure how to answer that, or even if he expected her to answer. Still, she found herself murmuring as soothingly as she could.

'I know Vivian would never have believed that. I'm sure there were plenty of others in the village who wouldn't have either—not the way they speak about you.'

'No, Vivian always supported me.' He balled up his fists tighter. 'She was the kind of foster mother that a kid like me could only have dreamed of having—well, you know that for yourself. If it hadn't been for her kindness, I've never cared to imagine where I might have ended up. Certainly not with the kind of lifestyle I have now. I know that for a fact. And how did I repay her? By never visiting? By resenting the fact that her illness meant I had no choice but to come back to this infernal place?'

'By all accounts,' Nell replied gently, 'you've flown Vivian all around the world—to any number of far-flung places, over the years.'

He turned sharply, his eyes boring into hers in the moonlight.

'You know about that?'

'Vivian is incredibly proud of the man you've become. She knows it was your way of thanking her—not that she ever needed thanks, I know—but she loved that you both got that time together to reconnect.'

'Perhaps, but I didn't do it often enough.' He pulled a face. 'I did it a handful of times over twenty years. I didn't really make the time for her that I could have made.'

'You made all the time Vivian needed.' Nell shook her head. 'Even if you'd wanted to do it more frequently, she couldn't have. You have to remember that she was still fostering other kids—*me*, for a start.'

'I suppose,' he began uncertainly. As if he hadn't actually considered it before.

'The first time you were able to fly her somewhere, Ruby and I were sixteen,' Nell pressed her point home. 'Vivian almost didn't accept because she was worried about us but we were so excited because the respite centre that would look after us was in the city. Two sixteen-year-olds spending a week in the big, exciting city—we convinced her that a mere seven days' holiday with you would be no time at all.'

'I hadn't even thought of that,' he acknowledged slowly.

'The second time you flew her somewhere—Mexico, I think, because she wanted to see the river where one of her favourite movie scenes had been filmed—Ruby and I were already at uni, and the two foster children she had were siblings who had just been able to return to their mother after her operation had been successful. There were similar circumstances for the other occasions she flew out to meet you, though I know she turned down quite a few over the years because you know how her foster kids always came first.'

'I do,' he admitted tightly. 'And I have to confess that I knew the fostering would prevent her from coming more often. I think I used it as an excuse not to keep regular contact.'

'You had your own reasons.' Nell shook her head, but Connor wasn't listening.

'I knew she hoped I would return to Little Meadwood to visit and I didn't want to keep letting her down so I was more than willing to accept the disconnect,' he bit out, clearly ashamed. 'It made it easier to put that less than palatable first half of my life firmly into my rear-view mirror. Ultimately, I drifted away—and Vivian cared about me enough to let me.'

He was so obviously beating himself up over it that it crushed Nell.

'She would hardly blame you if you had such unhappy memories of the place,' she reassured him.

'Except that I no longer even know if those memories are real, or if I just allowed a few individuals to taint my recollection of everyone else. Until you came along.'

'Me?' That part shocked her.

'You made me realise that I had some better memories buried inside. Deep down, perhaps—but there all the same. Flashes of images, or conversations, which make me wonder if not everyone had once been as hostile to me as I've always thought.'

'Memories like what?' she asked, going against every instinct she had not to push him too hard, or too fast.

She practically held her breath until Connor answered her.

'Such as the time the owner of the Willow Tree pub had given all the foster kids free jugs of orange cordial at the fairs, because he'd known they couldn't afford any of the home-made summer punch drinks on sale.'

'Yes, I remember that.'

'Well, I'd forgotten. I don't know how. Or one time when one of the older, kindlier farmers—not Lester Jones—had invited me to spend a few weeks on his farm learning how to be a cowhand one summer before he retired. I remember really enjoying it—the hard work, the learning—but until now I'd forgotten it all. Buried the good memories right along with the bad.'

'I suspect that's why Vivian pushed so hard for you to return here after all this time.'

Nell couldn't keep the smile from colouring her words, even as Connor shook his head.

'She couldn't have known.'

'Don't be fooled by Vivian's physical weakness.' Nell laughed affectionately. 'She's shrewder than you realise. It's why we love her. Why we've always loved her.'

And he just stared in silence for what might have been an entire age, before he finally conceded in a strangled voice.

'Perhaps that might be true, if only I knew what it actually means to *love* someone.'

And, in that moment, she finally understood what it was that had kept Connor constrained all this time.

'You think you aren't capable of love,' she realised aloud. 'Oh, Connor, of course you are. You love Vivian. You love life. You're more than capable of love.'

* * *

Connor was caught wholly off guard by Nell's declaration.

The certainty shone through her words like the brightest, hottest desert sun, filling him up and making him feel less hollow. Less empty.

She made him feel more whole than he thought he'd ever felt. More alive. Happy.

He wasn't entirely sure he deserved it. Yet he did nothing to stop her, just as he hadn't done anything to stop it these past weeks. He wanted so badly to believe her, and to be with her. Which was ridiculous because he didn't do that. He didn't do intimacy. He couldn't even bring himself to reveal his whole truth to her now.

'I'm not, Nell,' he bit out cautiously. 'Not real love, anyway. I want to, but I can't. I never have been capable.'

'Why would you say that?'

And the care in her words crept inside him like a velvet fist. It dug up the words he could never have found for himself.

'I guess I have no idea what it looks like. Aside from Vivian, no one has ever loved me—even Vivian came along when it was too late, when I was already broken. Damaged beyond repair.'

'That isn't true—' Nell began, but he cut her off.

If she was going to give her heart to him, as it had felt as if she was starting to do, and he wanted nothing more than to take it and cherish it for ever, then surely she deserved to know the real truth about him? To decide if he was worth it?

He suspected she would conclude that he wasn't.

He forced himself to continue.

'I was abandoned as a kid, Nell. My mother was a drug addict who would have happily sold me for a score—actually she *did* sell me for a score. Twice. And who knows who my father was? Probably the dealer she slept with in order to buy her drugs.'

'Connor...'

'I was left to fend for myself at the age of four. Probably younger.' He ignored her horrified interruption, too afraid that if she was too shocked he wouldn't be able to carry on. He had never told anyone the story about his past before. 'I don't even know how I survived as a baby—how she didn't just forget about me when she was on her benders. I think it was a neighbour who used to check on me until my mother accused her of meddling, and then we moved—if you can call it that.'

'What do you mean?' Nell gripped his arm tighter. He could almost have imagined she was trying to steal his pain away for him. And he loved... no, not *loved*...he was *grateful* to her for that.

Which only made him more of a liar.

'My mother schooled me to help her lie and steal from a young age,' he growled. 'I'd be the distraction while she took what she could: food, clothes, money. Then, when she went on one of her benders, I would fend for myself. I learned how to survive, and in that world there was no room for love. It was a weakness, something that could be used against you. So, I buried those feelings deep, convinced myself that I didn't need anyone, that I was better off alone.'

'You were just a kid,' she breathed, staring at him as if her heart were actually breaking for him. As if he were worthy of that kind of emotion.

'When I was six, my mother took us both to a motel where she was going to score. She locked me in the bathroom, and then she overdosed. That was when I ended up with Vivian.'

'I'm so, so sorry for all you've been through.' The feel of her delicate hand on his shoulder was pleasure and agony all at once.

'You don't have to feel sorry for me, Nell,' he ground out. 'I don't need your pity.'

He thought he was steeled against any reply she might make.

He was wrong.

'It isn't pity, Connor,' she told him softly. 'It's admiration. You've been through and coped with so much.'

'You can't admire someone like me,' he choked out. Shocked. Disgusted. Touched. He couldn't decide which.

'Too late. I already do.' She reached out to take his hand. 'But you need to know that you don't have to be alone any more. I'm here for you, always. And we can work through this together.'

And even as he opened his mouth to tell her that he didn't need that either, he found he couldn't say the words.

There was something else flowing through him that took a moment to pinpoint. Another moment to realise it was uncertainty. And the first flickering of hope.

'I...don't know if I can, Nell. I don't know if I'll ever be capable of love.'

But maybe, just maybe, he might be capable of something close, so long as he had someone like Nell by his side.

No, not someone *like* Nell. Nell.

Only Nell.

'You are, and you have so much love to give,' Nell countered, her voice gentle as her thumb rubbed softly against the fleshy part of his hand. 'You've proven that time and time again. When Vivian was sick, you gave up everything to be here for her. When I needed help with the fete, you immediately volunteered your services. You've been there for so many people, Connor. Don't you think it's time to let someone be there for you?'

Connor stared at her, turmoil twisting him inside out.

'I don't want to hurt you,' he whispered. 'I have so many regrets.'

'You know, you aren't the only one who is scared,' she whispered suddenly, and he couldn't say how he knew she hadn't known she'd intended to say anything until the words had already left her mouth. 'You aren't the only one with regrets.'

He swivelled his head then, his eyes searching hers.

'You? I thought you had a good childhood? Loving parents?'

'I did.' She swallowed tightly. As if fighting to get past some knotted ball that had just wedged itself in her throat. 'My parents were everything to me. But I…forgot it for a moment. Just at the worst time.'

'What happened, Nell?'

And it tugged at him that the concern that filled him was for her. As though she was right, and he really was capable of caring for her that much.

'I was thirteen and I'd just got my first boyfriend. They hated him. With hindsight, I can see exactly why—he was a rebel for the sake of being one, not because he truly believed in anything. He encouraged me to skip class to hang out down in the local town centre and busk for money instead.'

'You sang?'

'I played the violin. I was pretty good and I loved playing contemporary pop songs. He was using me, of course, using the money to buy cider, which he drank at the local bus stop, but I couldn't see it. I was just flattered by his attention, and desperate to have a boyfriend like the popular girls.'

'He doesn't sound worth it,' Connor growled, an unexpected fury raging through him at the idea of anybody using Nell like that.

'He wasn't. He certainly wasn't worth falling out with my parents over,' she agreed sadly. 'And I'd like to think I would have seen it for myself given just a little bit longer. But my parents stopped me from seeing him and I was devastated. I imagined myself in love. Thwarted. Like we were Romeo and Juliet. I told my parents that I hated them, and would never forgive them. I told them that I wished they weren't my parents.'

'Nell, you can't…'

She put her hand up to stop him. As though she was afraid she would never get the next words out if she didn't say them there and then.

'Less than a week later they were in the car accident that killed them.'

'Nell, I'm so, so sorry.' His arms were around her, drawing her in before he realised what he was doing.

Wishing he could go back in time and change it all for her. Even if that meant he would never experience the wonder of meeting a woman like Nell Parker. As if, maybe, there *was* a part of him capable of such deep feelings, after all.

And if there was, then it could only be because of her. Because Nell was the light, glorious and dazzling, and she belonged in Little Meadwood, where she called home. Whilst before her, he had always been him—broken and damaged. And, in that place more than any other, he would always be that cold, unwanted Mason kid.

But he didn't know what else to say. Or how to

explain it—even to himself. So, instead, he did the only thing he knew how to do—he kissed her.

Over and over.

Pouring everything he had into the moment. All the words he couldn't bring himself to think, let alone say. All these…*feelings* that he didn't know how to even begin to unravel.

As if Nell Parker was the only thing that could make this darkness inside him shift and skitter. As if he was running towards the light that this one, unique woman brought into his life. She flooded him with it, bright and brilliant as it illuminated all the better versions of himself that he wished he could be. For her.

And, for a while at least, he could pretend to himself that he really was that better man. Something he'd never wanted to believe in so much in his entire life.

CHAPTER ELEVEN

'APPARENTLY PEOPLE LOVE our steampunk stall,' Nell declared proudly as she bounced across the field, dodging the multitude of other fair-goers.

'Is that so?' Connor slid his arm around her shoulders as she pressed her side against his, falling into step together.

'Ruby swung by with Vivian, and she thinks they are the best stalls we've ever had. Plus, the mayor thinks we're going to have to make this a fixture every year.'

'Then I guess we have eleven months to work out how we're going to make it even better next year.'

She stopped, tilting her head to look up at him.

'So, you're sticking around Little Meadwood for a bit longer, then?'

Her lips parted, breathlessly, those morpho-blue eyes filled with such emotion.

Staying in Little Meadwood indefinitely had never really been part of the plan, yet right now he couldn't think of a single reason why he would refuse Nell. The past week with her had been incredible, whether they were working on the stall or at the hospital, or going on a date, or indulging in far more intimate pursuits. It felt as though this could be the start of something special—something he'd never before allowed himself to consider. And maybe they would have a long road ahead of them, but surely together they could make that journey?

'I'm considering it,' he hazarded, gently cupping Nell's chin with his hand as he lowered his head to kiss her.

A soft kiss but with so many unspoken promises. She tasted of goji berries and raspberries—that fruity fizz of her summer mocktail. She made him feel more alive, yet more grounded than any woman he'd ever known. The kiss deepened, but eventually he remembered where they were and reluctantly broke away.

'Later,' he managed, wondering how one word could be filled with such promise.

This was all so new and exhilarating to him.

'I might even move out of the hospital accommodation and rent an apartment of my own in the city. Between the army and locuming I've never actually had a place of my own before. And I might need some help decorating it. Though perhaps not steampunk.'

'Perhaps not.' Nell laughed, burying her head at his neck. A gentle rumble against his throat.

'I…' Connor opened his mouth to speak, only to realise that the words on the tip of his tongue were three words he had never, ever imagined wanting to tell anyone before.

He stopped abruptly, waiting for them to dissipate. Waiting for the sense of horror that he'd almost said something he could never mean. But it didn't come—even when she stood there, statue-still and staring at him with pupils so round that they were almost magical.

She was magical.

Perhaps it was those words still charging around in his mouth, hurtling themselves against his closed lips with such power that he almost couldn't hold them back any longer. Desperate to get out there into the world and be heard.

He loved her?

It seemed ridiculous. And impossible. And glorious.

'Connor…?' Nell breathed after what felt like a lifetime.

Perhaps it was.

'Connor?' she prompted again, her voice cracking. 'You…*what*?'

The silence swirled around them. Electric and exciting.

'I…' He faltered. But this wasn't the place to say it. Not here. Not at some summer fete in Little Meadwood. Ruthlessly shutting the errant thought out, he feigned a bright smile, which he suspected was a little too tight to look natural, and plucked her empty glass from her hands. 'I'll get us a refill.'

Without waiting for an answer, he turned his back and strode across the field to the drinks station. But the thoughts followed him. Prickling him. Making him feel *everything*.

'Another two Summer Suns, please,' he ordered, his head still lost.

He was still lost in his thoughts when he felt a sharp prod in his back. But when he turned, the smile on his face was wiped clean away.

'I don't know how you have the gall to come back here after what you did, my lad.' An unpleasantly familiar voice crackled through the air. 'You ought to be ashamed of yourself.'

He ought to have been shocked. It spoke volumes that he wasn't.

'Sylvie Calton.'

He fought to keep his voice level but even the old woman's name lodged unpleasantly in his throat. Sharp needles stabbing into the soft folds of his voice box like a prickly hawthorn into a soft thumb pad.

'It's Mrs Calton to you,' she hissed venomously, her gnarled features twisted in loathing. 'Or maybe *ma'am*. After all, you were supposed to be in the army, weren't you? I suppose Vivian knew it was either that or prison for the likes of you.'

'I don't know what you're talking about.' He refused to let this bitter individual transport him back to his sorry excuse for a childhood. He wasn't that kid any longer. 'But I can't say that I particularly care.'

If only there weren't that traitorous part of him

that did indeed care. Arguably for the way it might affect Nell more than himself.

'You know damn well what I'm talking about,' Sylvie spat out viciously. 'Vivian took you in when nobody else would. Like a fool, she treated you like her own son and wouldn't hear a word against you, even though I wasn't the only one concerned about how a feral monster like you would taint our happy community. And how do you repay her? By costing her all her life savings and then, when she *still* gave you another chance, you hurt her by running off like a coward. But I know what kind of a person you really are. And I'll never let you forget it.'

Connor's grip on the plastic cups tightened until they threatened to crack, but he was determined to keep his composure. He wouldn't let this woman win.

'I know exactly who I am,' he managed evenly, though it cost him. 'And I'm proud of who that is. As is Vivian.'

'You're a disgrace to a good woman. And you'll be a disgrace to her memory when she is gone.'

In hindsight, Connor would decide *that* was the moment he let Sylvie get to him.

'Why am I such a disgrace, Sylvie?' he gritted out, his voice low and dangerous.

'Because you're a liar, and a thief. Does that Nell Parker girl know what you are?'

Connor steeled himself. Nell being drawn into

anything in Little Meadwood was exactly what he'd feared.

'Nell knows,' he barked back. 'I told her all about the way I was dragged up, and how I used to survive. And do you want to know what Nell asked? She asked what was so startling about a six-year-old who was so desperate for his mother's love that he did exactly what she asked. Dragged up by a woman who hadn't even taught me the basics of right from wrong. I only learned that basic lesson when Vivian took me into her life.'

Sylvie's eyes glinted with pure malice.

'Oh, you might have pretended to learn that lesson, but we all know you were faking it. Just ask Vivian where her little nest egg went all those years ago.'

This time, he really didn't have any idea what she was talking about.

'Her nest egg?' He frowned, shocked, the cogs in his mind slipping as he tried to slot the accusation together.

Like a jigsaw puzzle with half the pieces missing.

Sylvie snorted in disgust.

'Don't pretend you don't know. Don't pretend you don't remember helping that wicked mother of yours steal hundreds of pounds from me.'

'That's a lie,' Connor scoffed instantly. 'I never saw that woman again after I arrived in this place to live with Vivian.'

'Yes. You did.' She prodded him in the chest, but he barely felt it.

'Ridiculous. She overdosed in a motel when I was six and that was the last time I ever saw her.'

Yet he couldn't explain the sudden heat that prickled through him.

'You can't really expect anyone to believe that you don't remember her coming here when you were about ten?' the old woman scorned. 'And you distracted me whilst she stole from me.'

'No.' He shook his head. 'I would remember.'

But things were still shifting hazily, and he didn't like the picture he thought they were making.

'Yes.' Sylvie sounded triumphant. 'You distracted me by paying for some toy with all pennies and tuppences. I ought to have realised then that was what was going on, but I'd foolishly bought into Vivian's version of you being a boy who had changed for the better.'

Connor felt winded. Waves of regret and remorse crashing over him. Threatening to wipe him out completely. He had been running from the pain for so long, but now it was catching up to him.

'I had no idea—' he began tersely, before Sylvie cut him off with a sneer.

'Of course you did. You distracted me whilst she stole. You knew. I saw you running after her afterwards, across the field to where some scrounger was waiting for her in some old car. Dusty red with a discoloured grey driver's door panel, I remember it like it was yesterday.'

And just like that, a memory dislodged itself from the darkest recesses of his brain. Buried so deep under guilt and shame that he'd forgotten it was there. He'd never wanted to see it again. His mother *had* tracked him down to Little Meadwood. How had he managed to stuff that memory down all these years? She'd given him the bag of copper pennies and told him to buy himself a toy like the ones she had never bought him. She'd claimed that she was clean and that it was her way of saying sorry for all she'd put him through as a child.

How desperately he'd wanted to believe her. Despite all the love and support Vivian had shown him, there had been that part of him that had still yearned for the love of the woman who was meant to be his mother. Who was meant to love him more than life itself. He'd seen other kids experience it—why not him?

So he'd taken the pennies from her and when she'd followed him into Sylvie's shop, he'd pretended that he hadn't known what she'd been planning. That he was still nothing more than her pawn. A part of him had known what she'd been about to do. And he'd let it happen because he'd felt this inexplicable sense of guilt. As though he had somehow left her all alone after her overdose. As if a social worker hadn't been the one to pack him in a car and take him to a home. Then to some foster family he could barely remember but who he knew hadn't been that kind. And finally to Vivian.

And when he'd got that toy—a bow and arrow set just like all the other boys in Meadwood had had, as if it had made him just like them—he'd chased the woman who had given birth to him but had never been any kind of mother across the green and begged her to take him with her.

And she'd laughed at him. Jeered. As if he was nothing.

'Who could love a runt like you?'

The words had echoed around his head for a lifetime. Worse, they had taken root. Because she hadn't been wrong, had she? He'd known what she was like yet he'd still allowed himself to be seduced by the idea that he was as worthy of love as any other kid. He'd allowed that desperate need to make him complicit in her crime against Sylvie, against Vivian, and against the trustworthy young man that Vivian had been trying to mould him into.

'I'm…sorry,' he managed. Simply. Sincerely.

He wasn't surprised when Sylvie merely sneered again.

'Excuses, excuses. You're a bad apple, Connor Mason. You were always a bad foster kid with a twisted, heartless soul. Always were, always will be, and the sooner you get out of here without causing damage for anybody else, the better. You even left it to Vivian to spend all of her savings paying me back.'

He ground out a curse.

'Well, someone had to pay me back, of course—but that someone should have been you. And then, a few years later, you ran off, abandoning her.'

Connor shook his head, guilt and shame knifing through him all over again. He had tried so hard to step away from his past, but he'd never thought he'd deliberately stuffed the truth out of his brain.

'I'm not the liar here, boy.' Sylvie couldn't have looked any happier with herself. 'You are. And you and I both know it.'

The accusation hung in the air, creating a heavy fog that threatened to engulf him whole. It was as if he were transported back to the days of his foster care. He could feel the hatefully familiar jagged edges of worthlessness and despair, feelings that had once consumed him. Only this time, he thoroughly deserved them.

He had spent twenty years fighting to escape Little Meadwood—fighting to be the best soldier, surgeon, man that he could be. He'd thought he'd finally escaped the feral kid he'd once been. He'd never wanted to feel like that scared, angry, worthless boy ever again. A boy who'd had nowhere to turn but inward—just as he felt as though he was doing now. He could turn himself inside out trying not to be that child, but he knew it wouldn't do any good. In the decade he'd endured living in Little Meadwood, the place had never allowed him to grow out of the feral six-year-old who had arrived, hissing and spitting like some wild animal, and he'd blamed the location and the people.

It turned out that the place wasn't the problem after all—he was. He always had been. And he'd been right in the first place in never returning here—it reminded him of the person he had never liked being.

A selfish, thoughtless individual who only cared about himself. Sylvie was right. He was a bad person and he didn't deserve love. He didn't deserve Nell or, more to the point, she deserved better than a man like him.

Emotions tumbled through Connor, too many and too fast to really identify any of them. Except for one.

Guilt.

Vivian had used up all her savings paying Sylvie back for his mother, so that she wouldn't go to the police. His mother had always been the one wrecking lives whilst he'd sworn he would never, *never* be like her.

Turned out, that was exactly who he was.

It was time for him to leave Little Meadwood before he caused any real harm. There was only one final loose end to tie up.

Nell.

A tight band pulled across his chest at the thought of her. Smart, compassionate, and full of integrity—all the qualities he'd once prided himself on possessing. Turned out he was just someone who was twisted and broken beyond repair. He had no love to give, no good qualities to offer, no one to keep him anchored. Not any more.

Nell deserved so much better—*someone* better. Not least someone who understood what it actually meant to love her back. This was his truth. He was a lost cause, and this was the only way to protect himself and those he cared about from the hurt and suffering he could cause.

The fact that he'd fallen for her—and he had—only made the thought of losing her that much more unbearable. It nicked at his heart.

Or what he had fooled himself into thinking was his heart. The truth was that he didn't have one. It had died long ago.

And it was time to make sure Nell understood that. For her own sake.

Nell reached Connor just as Sylvie was walking away. There was an odd gleam in the old woman's eyes.

'Connor.' She reached out to touch his arm, not entirely surprised when he pulled away. 'Whatever Sylvie said to you, forget it. You know she has always been spiteful.'

The woman had never been her favourite person here in Little Meadwood, although Nell could usually bring herself to feel a wave of sympathy for her.

'Doesn't make her wrong,' Connor bit out flatly,

and it was the lack of emotion in his tone that sliced through Nell painfully.

'I know she lost her son when he was just a baby, and I can't imagine how much pain that must have caused her, but that doesn't give her the right to treat other people as she does. What did she say to you?'

Connor's step almost faltered for a moment.

'Sylvie lost a child? I never knew that.'

'I think about forty years ago. I don't know much about it; I just know he was her only child.'

'That explains a lot,' Connor muttered, though Nell had the impression it was more to himself than to her. 'But it doesn't change anything.'

'What does that mean?'

He hated that he didn't answer.

'This is goodbye, Nell,' he forced out instead, still marching across the green.

'No,' she cried, almost falling. Connor was so wrapped up in whatever turmoil was clearly going on in his head that he hadn't even noticed she was practically tripping over the tufts of grass trying to keep up with him. 'What did Sylvie say to you, Connor?' she pleaded.

'It doesn't matter.'

And the flatness in his tone buried itself like a scalpel in her chest.

'Clearly it does,' she pointed out, relieved when he finally stopped and turned to face her.

'She simply reminded me of the person I really am. That's all. And I'm not the man you think I am.

I'm not even the man *I* thought I was. Frankly, I'm not a man worth knowing.'

'Too bad I've fallen for you, then, isn't it?'

And even as she uttered the words, she realised how true they were. Completely and utterly.

Connor stared at her for the longest time—a look that might have been dark and forbidding had it not been so very…compelling.

'Then you're a fool.' His voice grated.

'No…you love me too; you almost said it before. I know you did.'

He brushed her off and took a step away.

'I was wrong to think I was ever capable of love,' he dismissed, but it had the opposite effect to the one she suspected he intended.

It meant that he couldn't actually deny it. She was right, he *did* love her.

'Love is all that matters, Connor.'

She reached out to him, but he evaded her without even appearing to move. His teeth gritted so tightly that she almost expected his jaw to shatter under the pressure.

She almost expected *herself* to shatter under the pressure.

'That's a lie they sell you in movies, Nell. The truth is that love is not enough.'

'You're wrong.'

'Am I? Okay, then,' he challenged. 'If you love me so much, then come away with me.'

'Go away to where?' Her breath caught in her chest. 'You're leaving Little Meadwood?'

'Yes. And if you truly believe love is all that matters, then come with me. Leave this place, once and for all.'

The black look in his eyes almost reached down and suffocated her. He already knew she wouldn't be able to.

'You can't do it, can you?' He gave a brittle laugh after a few moments, and the sound seemed to echo coldly within her. 'Because no matter what you say, deep down you know that I'm not worth it.'

'No.'

That wasn't it at all, the problem was with her. She couldn't leave because this place was her safety net. Out there, in the real world, was where bad things happened. Like her parents dying. Jonathon had been right all along—she'd stayed in Little Meadwood for all the wrong reasons.

But she couldn't tell Connor any of that. She couldn't admit it out loud. She'd only just admitted it in the relative sanctity of her own head.

And so, he'd made up his own mind, and in *his* head, he was the villain. That was why he wouldn't stay.

'Don't go,' she pressed. 'You've got it all wrong. I may not know everything about your past, Connor, but I know you. I know the man you are today, and I love him. Whatever happened in your past, it doesn't define you. That isn't the man you are today.'

'You're wrong,' he gritted out. 'It moulds precisely the man I am today. The one standing right in front of you. And Sylvie reminded me how damaged, and how treacherous, that individual has always been.'

'Bruised,' Nell cut in desperately. 'Not *damaged* or *treacherous*. Just bereaved. Grieving for your parents. Like me.'

'Not like you,' he ground out. 'I was never like you.'

'Are you saying you never cared for me, Connor? That everything between us has been a lie?'

How she succeeded in keeping the quake out of her voice, she would never know. His expression was so black, so forbidding, that for a moment she feared he was going to say just that. But then something broke over his face. A glimpse of the tenderness that she recognised.

'That isn't what I'm saying.' There was a hint of anguish in his tone that gave her hope even as her heart broke for him. 'I cared for you… I still care for you. But that isn't enough.'

'It's enough for me,' she choked out.

'Then come away with me.'

It didn't even sound like an invitation. Just a test. One he knew she would fail again.

'This is ridiculous. We can't just leave Vivian,' she pointed out. 'Especially not now.'

‘I’ll visit,’ he stated flatly. ‘I’ll commute just like I did in the beginning. You can, too.’

She shook her head, her voice too thick to speak. The look he shot her held no surprise at all.

‘Ergo it isn’t enough,’ he said with finality. ‘Not for you. And not for me. It’s over—and I’m truly sorry about that, Nell. I never wanted to hurt you.’

And yet his expression was as implacable as his granite-like stance, making it abundantly clear to her that there was nothing she could say or do to help it thaw. He was lost to her.

If he’d ever really been hers in the first instance.

How could she have been so blind to the pain that he carried around inside him? Then again, how had she been so blind to her own self-imposed parameters? The boundaries she alone had created, which meant that even if Connor had been sincere about her leaving with him, she couldn’t have done so. This valley was her crutch, and she couldn’t face the idea of being without it.

Not even to be with Connor.

Which surely made her the one incapable of love—not him.

She’d told him she loved him but how could she really, when she couldn’t even face her own demons? How could either of them help each other when they couldn’t even help themselves?

And so, this time when he walked away from her—Nell simply let him.

CHAPTER TWELVE

CONNOR WORKED THROUGH the evening's patient notes in some kind of frenzy. The way that he had been doing for the better part of the past two weeks.

The past twelve days and twenty hours. He even knew it down to the minute—had anyone asked.

Though of course no one did. No one here knew him. He'd been fortunate that when he'd spoken with his chief of surgery at City, there had already been the option on the table of a month-long exchange with the general hospital on the other side of the city. It had meant being able to put some distance between him and Little Meadwood—and Nell—without anyone being left in the lurch. Not least his patients.

But even if he knew that staying away from Nell was the kindest thing he could do for her, it had to be the hardest thing he'd ever had to do in his life—including saving impossible lives in the most hellish warzones. How many times had he found himself on his motorbike in the middle of the night, screaming through the deserted country roads that led to the village? To her.

He'd always turned around before cresting that hill that overlooked the valley, though.

At least he had his work to get him through. It had always been his saviour.

Tonight alone, he'd already dealt with one patient who had fallen down a long flight of steep, concrete steps in town, fracturing his forearm. Despite the original X-ray from a colleague showing nothing, Connor's suspicions had led him to insist on a more comprehensive chest CT, which had revealed the full extent of the patient's injuries, resulting in a trip to the operating theatre.

He had then treated another patient who had been drinking too much, got into a brawl with his girlfriend, and then picked a fight with the plate-glass window of a high-street fashion chain and lost. Another quick dash to the operating theatre had ensued the moment he'd come in, and now the same patient was in ICU, the worse for wear, but alive.

He'd even performed a splenectomy on one road traffic accident victim, and removed half the severed pancreas of another. But now Resus was oddly quiet and even the non-trauma cases weren't enough to stop his brain from creeping back to Nell.

She'd taken up residency in his head and he couldn't seem to evict her, no matter what he did. He'd found himself looking for her in the hospital hallways, imagining he could hear an echo of her lilting tone in the corridor, or catch the faintest hint of her citrusy shampoo scent. Missing her in a way that he had never allowed himself to miss anyone before.

And he didn't want to feel any of it now. It made him feel too...*exposed.*

But worse, he suspected there was a tiny part of him that actually did want it. That might even like it. It was like nothing he'd ever felt before, and somehow that felt like a good thing.

Even so...when the door to his consultation room opened before he could respond to the brief knock, Connor knew it was her before she walked in.

He couldn't allow this to happen.

'Nell,' he rasped, lifting his head.

But the warning simply melted from his mind.

Standing in the doorway, wearing a simple figure-hugging tee, and a pair of inky-blue jeans, her hair pulled back into a loose ponytail, she was enough to snatch every last word from his head.

He didn't mean to sit up straighter in his chair, though Connor realised that was exactly what he was doing.

Somehow—he had no idea how—he managed to find his voice. A growl so dark that he barely recognised himself.

'You shouldn't be here.'

But rather than intimidating her into turning and fleeing as he wanted her to do—as he *needed* her to do—all Connor could see was a resolute glitter in her eyes. That inner strength of hers, which scraped at something inside him.

'Still self-flagellating, I see,' she offered dryly.

She seemed different…somehow. More sure of herself.

But he couldn't let that sway him.

'There's no punishment going on,' he growled again. 'I'm trying to spare you any hurt.'

'Only you're the one who is hurting the most,' she countered softly.

He shook his head, his words deserting him once again. And suddenly, there was no point still claiming that he didn't have a heart. Not when he could actually feel it right there, in his chest. Skipping a beat. The charged energy seeming to hum in the air around them.

But that still didn't mean he was capable of using it properly.

'I understand that you're scared,' she continued, stepping a little further into the room. 'But there's really no need to be.'

'I didn't walk away from you out of fear, Nell,' his voice rattled out oddly. 'I walked away because I'm not capable of love. I certainly don't love you enough to stay, just as you don't love me enough to leave.'

'You say that yet here we are.' She shrugged nonchalantly, her tone sending a wave of disquiet through him.

'Here we are?' he echoed, thrown.

It was a novel feeling.

'You claim you don't love me enough to stay, and I don't love you enough to leave, yet you haven't left,

Connor. You've moved a couple of miles further away, I'll grant you, but I'd hardly call that leaving.'

'Nell—'

'You haven't left,' she repeated, not letting him cut her off. 'And yet, I *have* left.'

'Sorry?'

It didn't help that Nell was far too cool, too unruffled, too at odds with the knot of feelings currently tumbling inside him. She exerted the kind of calm, composed energy that he usually prided himself on exhibiting, no matter the circumstance. But it had all deserted him right now, leaving him nervous and tense instead.

'You heard me, Connor.'

Only that pyretic lustre in her gaze offered any indication that Nell, *his* Nell, was less than controlled. Dimly, he considered that he should be using that to his advantage…so why wasn't he?

There were so many conflicting emotions inside him right now, all vying for pole position. He felt flustered, and apprehensive, and yet…the way his heart was racing inside his chest was almost like the kind of adrenalin rush to which he'd long since become addicted.

Almost, but not quite.

Because *this* sensation felt more tangible, more real. Which somehow made it all the more dangerous.

'What is it that you want from me?' he heard himself asking instead.

And that pounding in his chest only sounded louder, and harder, as she stepped further into the room. Into his space—which ought to have felt like an encroachment but instead felt oddly like someone pulling up a warm blanket on the coldest of nights.

Nell took a deep breath.

'I want you, Connor.'

'You do not want me.'

He didn't realise he'd launched himself to his feet until he heard his chair clattering to the floor behind him. A fist gripping inside his chest.

And Nell, damn her, merely smiled gently. With such understanding. As though she were trying to teach phonetics to a toddler.

'You can fight it all you want, but I've wanted you from the moment we met on that road outside the village. And I know you want me too.'

'I want no such thing.'

It didn't surprise him that the words sounded flat. Wrong.

She took another step closer.

'The difference is, you've finally given me the courage I needed to do something about it.'

'To do something about it?'

He was echoing her again. But his brain seemed to have stopped working.

'I've left Little Meadwood.'

'That isn't what—'

'I've sold my cottage.' She cut him off again.

And this time the simple statement was like a fist

in his chest, gripping so white-knuckle tight that it threatened to stop the blood in his very veins.

'You've sold your cottage?'

It sounded too unbelievable for words.

'I didn't want Little Meadwood to be my crutch any more—not when it was going to impede me chasing after you. And I understand why you're resisting—you had a hellish childhood, with only Vivian fighting for you. At least I knew loving parents and a warm family life before their accident. But you have more than one person now. You have me, too. I'm here, ready to fight for you. All you have to do is let me in. Let yourself feel.'

She made it sound so simple. So uncomplicated. But it wasn't that easy. It couldn't be. And the... *thing* that had festered inside him ever since he'd been that feral kid began to grow.

'I can't give you what you want,' he bit out. 'Even if I wanted to, I already warned you that I'm not capable of love. I never have been.'

'Yes, you are.' Her soft voice held such conviction that he ached to believe her. 'You've loved Vivian. You've shown love and care for your every patient. You've been part of a brotherhood in the military. That's love. It might take different forms but the trust, the loyalty, the promises are all there.'

He opened his mouth to argue but the words wouldn't come. Instead, a storm was beginning to howl through him, shaking his memories so that he couldn't even think straight.

Or maybe Nell was the storm.

Maybe she was the reason that the crashing in his ears only grew louder, as if a maelstrom were building up inside him with every comment this woman made, and it threatened to tear him apart, bit by bit.

'Even if that's true, it doesn't make me capable of…' he waved his hand between the two of them, as though to encompass all that he couldn't say '…this kind of love.'

Yet he barely recognised his own voice, it was so thick. So raw.

'It shows that you're capable of love after all.' Nell smiled softly.

He didn't answer. He couldn't.

His head was a mess of conflicting emotions, her words were like a balm to his soul, a soothing salve to the deep-seated pain that had been festering inside him for years.

Never before had he allowed anyone in—not even Vivian. Not fully. Just as never before had he allowed himself to feel vulnerable and exposed. But Nell was different, she made him want to take a chance and open up to her.

But if he hurt her?

Something nicked painfully at his chest as he realised that he would never be able to live with himself. It was all he could do to draw his next breath and steel himself.

'You're asking for something I can't give you,' he growled fiercely. 'You need to leave, Nell. Now.'

* * *

She had him. She could tell.

He didn't want to believe her—clearly, he thought that was the only way to protect her—yet her words were getting through. She kept catching flashes of turmoil in his dark eyes even as he tried to shut her out, as he had in the past.

'Pity, since I'm choosing to stay.' Somehow—she didn't know how—Nell managed to crank up her smile, wander over to the sleek leather couch at the side of his office, and sink down with a nonchalance that she only wished she really felt. 'So you can glare and glower at me all you want. You can rail and storm. But it won't induce me to apologise for acknowledging my feelings.'

'Then you are only fooling yourself if you think it will induce *me* to share them.'

She noted how he deliberately echoed her words, trying to turn them back on her. And that, too, fuelled her.

'I think it's time we stopped going around in circles, Connor.'

And her stomach somersaulted again as she watched the way he curled his fists around the edges of his desk, fighting for his own self-control as much as anything else. She was clearly getting under his skin.

Good.

'I've come to fight for us,' she told him soberly.

'To show you that I love you. That you can trust me. That I will always have your back.'

And she would never know how her voice didn't shake with the intensity of emotions roiling around inside her at that moment.

'Then you're a fool. It isn't a battle worth having.' His jaw clenched and for a moment Nell thought that he was going to walk away.

But then he surprised her by stepping around the desk. Still on the other side of the room from her, but without that physical barrier, at least.

It was a start—even if he was simply staring her down with a fierce intensity that made her heart race. If time had stood still—the rest of the world grinding to a halt around them—then she wouldn't have been shocked.

The only thing that existed for her in that moment was her and Connor.

'You aren't defined by your past,' she managed, after what might have been an eternity. Maybe longer. 'You're defined by who you are now, and who you want to be. I'm not going to let you push me away this time, Connor.'

For a moment, there was silence between them, and Nell thought that she had said too much. But then he spoke, his voice hesitant, and rough.

"You have no idea what you're asking for.'

'I'm just asking for love, Connor,' she whispered. 'Nothing more complicated than that.'

'I don't know if I can be what you deserve.' But

his voice cracked. Right there. Right then. 'I don't know if I'm capable of loving someone the way that you deserve to be loved.'

'You won't know unless you try,' Nell said, her voice gentle.

The air between them was electric, charged with the unspoken tension that had been building between them for weeks. Nell could feel the heat emanating off Connor's body, could see the way his pupils dilated as he watched her.

Desire.

Potent enough to make her insides begin to melt and flow through her. Thick, and warm, and thrilling.

And then, suddenly, he was crossing the room. Closing the space so quickly that she barely had time to react, much less think. He reached out his hand to take hers and pulled her to her feet and right up against his hard, lean body.

Like coming home.

'I've missed you,' he muttered, before lowering his head to claim her lips with a kiss that made her feel as though a dam had burst inside her.

As if someone had set off a thousand fireworks throughout her entire body.

A kiss that was hungry and desperate, as if trying to make up for lost time. Yet was also infused with every unspoken promise that she could ever have wanted. As if he was finally letting go of his fears and insecurities and allowing himself to fully embrace the passion and desire that he had been suppressing for so long. Pouring his soul into that kiss. Into *her*.

And Nell soaked up every bit of it.

Every seductive slick of his tongue was a silent avowal, every deepening angle an admission of need. When his hands roamed her body, Nell couldn't stop the soft moan from escaping her lips as her hands came up to tangle in his hair.

They stood there for what felt like an eternity, lost in the intensity of their passion, until finally they pulled away—Connor's forehead resting against hers as his ragged breathing mingled with hers.

'I can't promise that this will be easy; but I want to try.'

'That's all I ask,' she promised him, her fingers reaching up to stroke his cheek. 'Because I love you. And you don't have to say it back; I understand why you can't yet allow yourself to accept that you love me too. But I can wait. I can love you enough for the both of us. Until you're ready.'

'And if I never am?'

'You will be,' she told him confidently, his ragged breath spurring her on. 'You already feel it, you just have to recognise it.'

And as they stood there, wrapped up in each other's embrace, their gazes intertwined, Nell saw the exact moment Connor finally believed her. The moment his fractured shield finally shattered and fell away. His body told her the truth even if he hadn't yet found the courage to say the words. Every gaze, every touch, every kiss proved he loved her better than any promises could have done. Because anyone could say the words, but no one had ever made her feel the way that Connor did.

'From that first day we met, it was like you shone a light into my life when I'd never before known how dark it was,' he told her solemnly, his gaze full of wonder. 'And then, as I got to know you, I realised you weren't shining a light—you *are* the light. A blazing, dazzling sun that has breathed a life into me that I never imagined I could be. I *do* love you, Nell. I think I always have. I just didn't know what it meant.'

'Now you do,' she whispered, her heart swelling with emotion. So much that she thought it might burst out of her chest.

'I swear to you,' he continued, his voice cracking, 'that I will spend every day striving to be the man you deserve. Telling you how much I love you. And proving it to you.'

'I think we should start on all of that right now,' she agreed, lifting her hands to trail her fingertips down the sides of his face.

And then she half laughed, half cried as he scooped her into his arms, hauling her against his chest whilst his mouth came down to seal his promise.

'I love you, Nell,' he murmured, laying her almost

reverently on the couch. 'You are my light, and my life, and you deserve to be worshipped. For ever.'

Then he bent his head and began to do precisely that, stripping her down one item of clothing at a time, and stoking the fire that burned so white-hot between them. And Nell knew they were like two pieces of a puzzle that finally fitted together, completing each other in the most perfect way.

The way they would for the rest of their lives.

* * * * *